# HER LOST WORDS
# HER BROKEN SILENCE

*SHANTANEL PAYNE*

Printed in the United States of America.

ISBN:

First Printing, 2020

Shreveport, LA 71109

## CHAPTER 1: New Beginnings

As the wind blew in Summer's face, she inhaled and smiled, knowing that she was traveling to an opportunity of new beginnings and endless possibilities. Finally, she had a purpose in her twenty-two years of being on this earth. As she traveled to her new destiny and took in the new scenery, she wondered what her new job would offer. Would she have a difficult time fitting in? Could she actually accomplish this on her own? Despite trying to maintain positive thoughts, her past of loneliness, fear, and feeling unwanted kept creeping in.

Summer Taylor's journey began at age three when she was found in an abandoned drug house on the south side of Jamaica Queens, New York. She became an orphan, a ward of the state, until she reached the age of emancipation, as she was never adopted and remained in a group home until she turned eighteen years old. Her parents remained a mystery to her.

As a child, Summer struggled in the group home. She never had a voice; therefore, she was always soft-spoken and shy. Kids often picked on her because she was an easy target.

Amidst the challenges of her childhood, Summer found an unexpected ally in Miss Dangerfield, the cafeteria supervisor. Miss Dangerfield's nurturing presence became a beacon of hope in Summer's life, showing her the power of mentorship and the difference a caring adult can make in a child's life.

Summer could close her eyes and still recall the comforting scent of Miss Dangerfield's sweet perfume, the gentle rocking motion as she held her close, and the encouraging words that urged her not to let the other kids walk all over her.

Miss Dangerfield, in a selfless act of kindness, as Summer's situation tugged so deeply at her heart, would discreetly slip an extra lunch bag to Summer every day during the week before leaving the facility. This ensured that Summer had enough to eat throughout the night and on weekends when she was off. A testament to Miss Dangerfield's unwavering care for Summer, knowing she had adjusted her mindset to go without and was too afraid to speak out. The impact of Miss Dangerfield's actions was not just in the food but in the sense of care and belonging it brought to Summer's life.

Summer would sneak into her secret hiding place on the weekends, where she would remain until her presence was requested. She learned to pass the time by reading any books she could get her hands on as she escaped from her reality by living through the characters in the books she read. She avoided making friends as most of the kids who were friendly to her got adopted out. She quickly learned not to get emotionally attached to any of the kids.

Miss Dangerfield was the only consistent person in her life. Although she longed for a better life, she soon accepted that the confinement behind the group home's walls was her reality. Thus, the scent of lead paint blended with musty odors, and a worn-down twin mattress became her everyday norm.

Miss Dangerfield became the only mother figure Summer would ever know. She took her in when she turned eighteen and ensured that Summer completed high school and graduated from college with her BSN in nursing. Summer was driven by her unyielding determination to make a difference and work in an area where her duties served a greater purpose. It didn't take long for her to find employment after graduating from nursing school. Surprisingly, she fit in well at her new job. In fact, she was astonished when her boss recommended that she transfer out of state to their sister hospital in Springfield, Illinois, after only being a new charge nurse on her unit for six months.

Summer initially hesitated to accept the job offer, knowing it meant leaving behind Miss Dangerfield, the only family she had ever known. However, Miss Dangerfield's words convinced her that this was the perfect opportunity to begin a fresh start and begin living, which held a powerful sway over her. So, with great apprehension, Summer finally decided to accept the job offer.

As a child, she had never experienced life outside the walls of her group home. She attended boarding school until the age of eighteen. After that, she started taking college courses and lived off campus in a small two-bedroom house that she shared with Miss Dangerfield. It felt like a mansion in her mind, as she had never had her own bedroom before.

She had a daily ritual of disengaging herself from her peers. Instead of embracing college life and mingling among her peers, she spent most of her day with her head in a book or hiding behind the bleachers, watching the band. She was captivated by the performances of the band and drum majors, developing a deep passion and interest in their practice sessions. Despite her own fears, she admired their courage to perform in front of thousands at a college game, a feat she could never imagine herself doing.

At the tender age of twenty-two, Summer had yet to experience the simple joys of holding hands or sharing a kiss with someone of the opposite sex. She would often self-consciously sabotage her outer appearance, which brought little to no attention to her.

A fun day out for her consisted of shopping for fabric with Miss Dangerfield to make clothes and ending their outing with a chocolate-coated ice cream cone from Mr. Pete's ice cream parlor.

Their conversation rarely touched on male or female friends. Instead, they reveled in the day, finding solace and joy in their unique bond.

Summer knew that her upcoming journey wouldn't be easy. She had no prior life experience and had never been on her own, so it would be a significant challenge to embrace. The only physical affection she had ever received was in the form of sweet forehead kisses from Miss Dangerfield. She had never been romantically involved with anyone, nor had she ever received attention from a guy. So, she would be a fish out of water as she embarked on her new journey.

Summer also lacked fashion sense, often taking tips from a 64-year-old black Jehovah's Witness, which didn't help land her on the best-dressed list. Although Summer was a beautiful and intelligent young woman, her college classmates described her as a "Coke bottle body in a burlap sack." They simply referred to her as a friendly, curvy woman who hides her shape with oversized, unflattering clothing. She just couldn't seem to embrace herself enough to fit in with her peers.

Finally, an opportunity came for her to branch out and discover herself. This opportunity not only pushed her into purpose, but it also pushed her into being a responsible young woman who was taking control of her life. With Miss Dangerfield gifting her a new vehicle and a free apartment provided by her job for the first six months of her relocating, Summer had no excuses not to succeed on this new journey.

*** 

Summer felt her heart racing as the GPS counted down the miles. She was afraid to walk in her new grown-up shoes, and her mind immediately started racing with thoughts of failure. Flashes of that lonely child being fearful of her surroundings flooded her mind. She became so overwhelmed with panic that she pulled over and called the only person who could talk her through this.

"Mimi," she cried out when Miss Dangerfield answered the phone. "I can't do this. I just want to come home."

Miss Dangerfield replied sternly, "Hush your fuss. This is God's destiny for you, my child. Now, you stop crying and pull yourself together."

Summer knew in her heart that she had to accomplish this next step in her life. Her commitment to prove herself to Mimi was like a heavy burden on her shoulders. She was determined not to let Miss Dangerfield down. Her only true goal at that moment was to prove to Mimi that her hard work and dedication to her were not in vain.

Summer gathered herself and continued her journey. Without any more procrastination, she arrived at her new job site. She had instructions to meet with the recruiter to receive the keys to her new apartment and to take a tour to review the new facility. With determination, she dashed out of the car while saying a loud prayer in her head in an attempt to drown out the negative thoughts that had plagued her throughout her entire life.

As she walked into the building, attempting to feel proud and confident, she made her way to the recruiter's office, Stevin Bash. Her heart started beating a little faster with each step she took. She stalls at Mr. Bash's office door to compose herself before she shoots right into his office. As she approached Mr. Bash to introduce herself, he immediately stood and walked from around his desk to shake her hand. In typical Summer fashion, she was only focused on looking the part and never noticed Stevin's strikingly attractive appearance. Here stood a tall, dark, and handsome Italian man, a very nice cut guy three feet away from her, and all she could think was, 'Stare at his forehead as if you are making eye contact without actually making eye contact. I wonder if he can tell I am nervous. I pray he's not having second thoughts about hiring me.' Her self-doubt was overwhelming, and it was a struggle to keep it at bay.

After the introduction and brief banter, Stevin escorted Summer on the tour. As they walked and talked about the office and the company, a staff meeting was called to introduce her to everyone. Summer's surprise was palpable when she learned that she was not only walking into a new position but would also be the new nurse supervisor for the new cardiac care unit. The news hit her like a thunderbolt, and she struggled to maintain her composure. She was too afraid to speak out, and her legs trembled under the table. She was screaming silently inside, "NO! NO! This is not right. I'm not trained in this area." Despite feeling like she was dying inside, yet her outward appearance said differently.

She sat quietly through the meeting, her professional facade in place with her head held high and her shoulders back, trying to look the part. However, the physical manifestation of her nervousness was undeniable- her heart was racing in her chest, a clear sign of her inner turmoil. At that moment, she was certain that she had made the biggest mistake of her life.

Finally, the meeting adjourned. As Summer walked out, she appeared confused and shaken up. Mr.

Bash noticed the nervous look on Summer's face. He smiled and assured her that everything would be okay.

"It's okay. You will do fine. We have heard great things about your work ethic. You will fit in just fine," he assured her.

He further explained that she would go through six weeks of training and would have plenty of time to learn the unit and her new role. Summer sighed in relief. Then, he handed her a $25,000 incentive check for relocating. The sight of the check, the largest sum of money she had ever seen in her life, sent her heart racing. At that moment, she felt a surge of empowerment.

The next item on the agenda was to view her new apartment. She followed the recruiter in her car to her first new place of residence, which she had acquired on her own. As they drove from the office to her place, Summer took in the scenery. She was still in awe of her surroundings before realizing they had arrived at her new home. Her jaw dropped as they pulled into a luxurious gated apartment complex, a sight that left her speechless. She admired the grand water fountain and the meticulously landscaped surroundings, which looked like a scene from a movie. As both cars parked, Summer noticed the reflection of the clear, crystal blue water from the swimming pool beaming off the windows of the clubhouse. She immediately felt the Globus sensation in her throat from holding her breath to avoid crying.

When the recruiter attempted to exit his vehicle, Summer stopped him.

"Just point me in the direction of my apartment. I've already taken up enough of your time today."

"Summer was a whirlwind of emotions, a mix of excitement, fear, and nostalgia. The milestone of stepping foot in her own apartment was a moment she wanted to experience alone. Besides, she knew Mr. Bash wouldn't understand why she'd be choked up behind a swimming pool and landscaping.

As the recruiter started to pull off, he asked, "When will your furniture arrive? The apartment isn't furnished."

Summer smiled and said, "It's fine. I promise you, I will be okay."

The recruiter's expression softened a hint of understanding in his eyes.

Yet, as she mentally exclaimed, "Well, shit! I didn't think of that." In the midst of preparing for her new life, furniture was the furthest thought on her mind.

Attempting not to look like a deranged psychopath in the parking lot, she spun around in circles, taking in her new surroundings.

Her new home was a far cry from the white walls of the one-bedroom, twelve-bed group home she had known all her life. As she rushed up the stairs to apartment 22B, she paused and realized that the swimming pool would be a constant sight from her apartment.

Summer was filled with excitement to hear the clicking sound of the deadbolt lock turning while she twisted the key to unlock the door. Opening the door, she was met with a cool breeze from the AC that hit her face, and the smell of fresh paint, a sharp and refreshing scent, traveled through her nostrils. Tears streamed down her face as she dropped to her knees, overwhelmed with emotions. She immediately began to think back to that lonely kid she once was, never imagining she would have a reason to smile. Curling up into a fetal position on the floor, she took in the moment to soak it all in. Laying her face on the carpeted floor, she could feel the carpet fibers against her cheek. Her thoughts were interrupted by the sound of her ringing cell phone, prompting her to jump up and grab it.

"Hello... Mimi! You won't believe it! My apartment is absolutely amazing!" I'm so excited!" she exclaimed as she walked around, feeling the granite countertops and describing the apartment.

"I have a fireplace and a washer/dryer unit too! Mimi, my patio overlooks a big, beautiful pool!" She continued with excitement as she discovered these features along with Miss Dangerfield.

As she made her way to the bedroom, the realization hit her like a ton of bricks-she had no bed, no food, not even a face towel. She continued enlightening Miss Dangerfield on her experiences so far and sought her advice. Then, she abruptly ended the call, informing her that she needed to rush to the store before darkness fell. Miss Dangerfield quickly went over the dos and don'ts before hanging up.

As Summer made her way out the door, she suddenly found herself face to face with her neighbor, who had just stepped out of his apartment and greeted her. "Well, hello, sweetie. How do you like your new apartment?" he asked.

Summer was immediately overcome with a wave of unease as nausea churned in her stomach. The pungent stench of his cologne was a stark reminder that she had been too anxious to eat and had not eaten all day. The overbearing neighbor loomed as he followed her to the car.

"My name is Mr. Ben. I have lived here for ten years. Just let me know if you need anything. Anything, I said."

"Thank you," replied Summer as she rushed to close the car door.

She breathed a sigh of relief as she pulled off and watched Mr. Ben's reflection disappear from her rearview mirror. She used her GPS to find the nearest Walmart. Before she knew it, three hours passed before she made her way to the checkout lane. As she struggled to steer her overloaded cart to the cashier, Summer found herself completely drained. She had shopped until her cart couldn't hold any more items. She had picked up anything, and everything she thought might be useful and placed it in the cart. She'd always shopped with Miss Dangerfield and always needed what Miss Dangerfield needed. With no clear desire of her own, it never dawned on Summer that the most she had splurged on in her life were drinks from the concession stand at the movie theater instead of sneaking in Kool-Aid Jammers and Capri Suns in Miss Dangerfield's oversized purse.

After loading the bags into her car with no room for anything else, she quickly realized that she would have to unload her car and walk up a flight of stairs when she arrived back at her apartment building.

She conquered the feat by tiptoeing in and out of her apartment, hoping to avoid another encounter with Mr. Ben. After several trips, she finally got the last grocery bag and her suitcase out of her car. Just one suitcase. It contained everything she owned except for a framed photo of her and Miss Dangerfield.

After a tiring day, she felt grateful that it was Friday, and she had the entire weekend to get adjusted. Once she finished putting away her groceries, she placed her only family photo on the mantelpiece above the fireplace. Then, she removed her queen-sized air mattress from its box and connected the pump to blow it up in the middle of her living room. As her temporary sleeping arrangement filled with air, she couldn't help but smile and walked around her apartment. She walked to the window and pulled the blinds open, revealing the crystal blue waters of the swimming pool outside the window, muttering to herself, "A perfect view."

Finally, with a deep sense of relief, she ended her day. She took a soothing bath and went to bed for the first time in her own home, feeling a wave of peace and comfort wash over her.

# CHAPTER 2: Breaking Old Habits

Three weeks in, and Summer soon learned that she was fitting in fine. She continued the daily routine that she had followed since being in the foster care system. She awakened at 5:00 a.m. to shower. Then, she enjoyed half an English muffin and a cup of hot tea for breakfast. She continued her morning routine by completing chores that she commanded of herself. She welcomed a sense of routine. Only having furnished her apartment with a bedroom set, a dinette table, and two bean bags in her living room with a twenty-inch TV, her morning chores only consisted of making her bed and vacuuming before heading off to work.

Summer stuck to her usual routine when it came to her appearance - she wore oversized nursing scrubs, tied her frizzy hair back in a sleek ponytail, and went makeup-free. However, her dull external appearance didn't hinder her newfound confidence at work. She was loving her job, with the exception of some eye-rolling from certain staff members who felt they deserved her position. It didn't take long for her to find her voice and embrace her role as a member of the team - a team that she was actually in charge of.

Finally, things had taken a turn in her life. She blocked out the fact that she remained alone. The only thing she had to look forward to was immersing herself in her work and going home to the beautiful view of the swimming pool that she so loved to stare at for hours.

One afternoon at work, Summer was sitting at her desk when she heard a tap on her office door. A voice said through the slightly ajar door, "It's me… Stevin." The recruiter, Mr. Bash, had made a special trip to her office to see how she was coming along in her new position. As she reassured him that she was catching on fairly quickly, she noticed that Stevin had made his way into her office. As they stood face-to-face, something about today's visit seemed different. In typical Summer behavior, she was completely oblivious to any signs that involved someone from the opposite sex could actually be interested in her, her innocence shining through.

Stevin was now standing at arm's length, hovering about, smiling big, and making eye contact as if he was hanging on to every word Summer spoke. There was clearly some flirtation on his part; still, Summer ignored all signs. Used to being overlooked and still on her mission of self-consciously sabotaging, she missed the thought that Stevin could possibly be into her. As she attempted to walk him out of her office to the elevator, her only focus was to get him out of her office so she could get back to the pile of papers on her desk.

As they approached the elevator, Mr. Bash stopped and turned to face Summer, asking if she would like to have drinks with him and some other coworkers after her shift ended. However, she declined the offer, swiftly retreating back into her office to immerse herself in the piles of files on her desk. It never occurred to her that she actually turned Stevin down or that it might have been possible that he found her attractive.

Summer had become acquainted with a staff member named Ebony Holmes. Ebony was very easygoing and had gone out of her way to ensure that Summer had a smooth transition. Summer hesitates about crossing boundaries and wants to ensure their relationship remains professional. She personally didn't want to get too close with her staff members outside the office. Nevertheless, having someone to talk to and relate to for a change was refreshing. Summer appreciated Ebony's sense of humor. Unfortunately, she brought along baggage by the name of Amber Ross. She was another nurse on the unit and Ebony's best friend. Amber was an eye-rolling snooty bitch who felt entitled to Summer's position. It was rumored that she attempted to sleep her way to the top by having sex with the Chief Resident. Nevertheless, Summer remained professional and never gave in to the urge to spike her drink with a little of her saliva when she was not looking.

Amber loved to tag along at lunchtime and made sure to do everything possible to make Summer feel unwanted. However, being unwanted and enduring others' dislike and mistreatment was Summer's norm. She had made a deal with herself that as long as Amber did her job, she would overlook the eye-rolling and snooty attitude.

Summer sat quietly daydreaming as Amber ambushed the lunch, taking over the conversation with her obnoxious storytelling about her weekend dating fling. Summer sat thinking back to her childhood, when she was afraid to talk and was bullied by other kids who threw food at her, calling her "The Mute Imbecile." She thought back to when she was five years old, her first opportunity to be adopted. She remembered looking up and staring into the eyes of the lady who could have been her mom.

The beautiful woman, her face a picture of patience, gently stroked her cheek and asked, "Hello there, sweet child. What is your name?"

Summer was on the edge of her seat, frozen in the moment of excitement, screaming silently in her mind, "Summer, new mom! My name is Summer!"

But no words would come out. Summer's voice was trapped in her throat, struggling to break free. Before Summer could muster up the courage to speak, the lady's husband stepped in front of her, turning her beautiful bright light of sunshine rays into a dark shadow. He was screaming repeatedly, "Pick another one. We want another child. This one is retarded. She doesn't speak."

Immediately frightened, Summer became incontinent, wetting herself. At that moment, she could remember the lady being swept away. She was only able to see her shadow as her husband stood like a dark cloud, blocking her view. That day was the first memory of the cafeteria lady with the sweet-smelling perfume coming to her rescue. As Miss Dangerfield helped her clean herself up and put on fresh clothing, Summer received her first gentle hug of compassion from Miss Dangerfield. She found instant comfort and felt protected in that hug. It was a moment of psychological ease, temporarily removing her for just a moment from the hardships she faced day in and day out. Summer would have multiple opportunities in her teen years to be adopted, but because of the strong bond that she had developed with Miss Dangerfield, she learned quickly how to sabotage any potential adoption.

As lunch ended and they returned to the unit, Ebony turned to Summer and said, "Oh, Summer, I forgot to tell you I will be having a girls' night this Saturday. I would love for you to come."

Before Summer could reply, she noticed Amber in the distance behind Ebony's head, rolling her eyes with a twisted and mean look on her face. Amber was making it very clear that she was displeased with the invitation from Ebony. Summer, adept at handling such social cues, ignored her rudeness yet again as she was more focused on quickly turning down Ebony's offer. She was thinking to herself, "I better not accept the offer. What would I say if she ever wanted to come to my apartment?" She quickly reminded herself that she only had two bean bags for her guests to sit on. Summer politely declined Ebony's offer. She promptly returned to her office, logged on to the internet, and ordered living room furniture with the click of a button.

After traveling down memory lane during lunch, Summer felt an overwhelming desire to see Miss Dangerfield. She decided to give her a call.

"Hello," Miss Dangerfield answered.

"Mimi," Summer replied with excitement in her voice.

She quickly began ranting about Amber and her dislike for her. Miss Dangerfield promptly reminded Summer she was not in that position to be everyone's friend. She encouraged her to attend Ebony's gathering and to maintain a professional distance from Amber.

"Mimi!" Summer yelled in a high-pitched voice. "I know what! How about you come down for the weekend? I can purchase your airline ticket tonight."

Miss Dangerfield so gracefully declined with a weak, shaky voice.

"But why not, Mimi?"

Miss Dangerfield explained that she had been under the weather with a head cold. She said she would be more than happy to fly out once her sinus issues cleared up. Summer ended the call, promising Miss Dangerfield that she would try to get out of the house this weekend to enjoy herself.

Summer immediately located Ebony to inform her that she would be attending her get-together. Ebony told her the theme was a slumber party, and she needed to wear pajamas.

Summer squealed, "I have to drive over in night clothes?"

Ebony giggled and replied, "Yes, ma'am. You do."

Summer thought to herself, 'When I get off, I will just go to Walmart and pick up some plaid flannel pajamas.' In her mind, a long-sleeve button-up plaid shirt with matching pants would cover her up just fine.

## CHAPTER 3: Excited About Shopping

As Summer walked into Walmart, she was nearly skipping with excitement—the idea of finally shopping for an event she had been invited to overwhelmed her with joy. Besides, Miss Dangerfield had encouraged her to go, and it would be a joy to Mimi's heart when she called to tell her how much fun she had. The thought of sharing this experience with Mimi filled her with warmth and anticipation. When she turned down the aisle of women's sleepwear, there it was, shining like a diamond - an all-over pink flannel pajama suit. Summer was in awe.

"Just perfect! Just perfect...," she repeated. She knew it was a clear sign that it was destined for her to be at the party. Skipping along throughout the store, she meticulously picked up a pink bandana for her head and even lucked up and found some pink fluffy booties. Summer had it all planned out. On top of that, she came up with a new hairstyle. She thought, "I'll part my hair down the middle and do two pigtails with my pink bandana tied around my head. Oh my! I'm going to be such a bad chick at this party that Amber won't know what hit her." She also picked up some Carmex lip balm so she could make her lips pop.

Filled with excitement, Summer couldn't wait to share with Ebony. She sent her a text: "I'm so excited about Saturday. I found the perfect outfit." Ebony quickly replied, "Lady, what did you buy? And most importantly, where did you purchase your outfit from?"

Summer replied, "I'm not sharing." She thought to herself that she hoped nobody would show up wearing the same thing, so she ended the text by saying, "You are going to love my pajamas. I can't tell you what I'm wearing because you might copy me. Lol."

As she pulled into her parking space, she was still smiling and thinking about how lucky she was to find the perfect outfit. Her smile quickly turned into a frown when she saw Super Mack from the '70s, aka Mr. Ben, standing in her assigned parking place dressed in all gold. He had on so much gold that her headlights were beaming off his large gold rope necklace that dangled around his neck. Before Summer could park, Mr. Ben was walking to her car window, revealing a rose behind his back.

"I've been waiting for you. I'm running late. I almost called the police," he said.

With a confused look, Summer asked, "Why did you almost call the authorities?"

"You see here... I figured you get off at 5 o'clock because you're normally home around 5:30 p.m.," he explained. Summer was still at a loss for words, debating if she should push him down and just start running. Mr. Ben, realizing that he had startled her, suddenly became aware and worried his actions might have frightened her. He started clearing his throat, mumbling, and stuttering his words, attempting to make amends for his sudden approach.

"You see… You see. I can hear when you come in. I'm not watching you. I promise I'm not watching."

Mr. Ben started sweating and pulling at his necklace as if he were having trouble breathing. Seeing his distress, Summer was afraid that he was about to hyperventilate and pass out, and images of her having to give him mouth-to-mouth quickly changed her demeanor. She touched his arm and changed her tone.

"Calm down, Mr. Ben. Why were you waiting for me? What did you need?"

"Baby girl, you see, I was invited to my friend's barbeque, and I wanted you to attend it with me. I never see anyone over, and I wanted you to come out and enjoy yourself."

"Mr. Ben, that's very sweet of you, but I've had a long day, and I'm exhausted. Besides, waiting for me has already made you late. I don't want to hold you up any longer."

Mr. Ben persisted, "Are you sure? We can knock them dead walking in arm-in-arm."

Summer exited her car. "Yes, Mr. Ben, I'm sure."

## THE WEEKEND IS HERE

Saturday morning arrived, and Summer had been up since 5:00 a.m. She sat on her bean bag, staring out at the pool as if she was watching the ocean. Summer was excited about today - not only would she attend her first party, but she was also awaiting the arrival of her new furniture.

Since she ordered everything online, she had no idea if everything would fit properly. Suddenly, she heard a tap at the door. It was the delivery guys with her furniture. She signed for the delivery, and they began moving everything in. As the two delivery guys wrestled to get the first piece of furniture in, Summer looked up and was surprised to see that Mr. Ben had finessed his way into her apartment, holding a sofa cushion.

He said, "I can help, gentleman if you'd like." Then, he turned to Summer, "What have you been sitting on? I've been up all morning, and I haven't seen you move any furniture out."

Summer smiled. She had accepted that Mr. Ben was no threat - only a nosey neighbor.

One delivery guy asked, "How would you like us to set the furniture up?"

Summer replied, "Just set it down however you'd like."

Mr. Ben looked at Summer and shook his head. "No, child, we can't have that."

He sprang into action, barking orders, moving furniture, and even having the delivery guys reposition the dinette table.

Summer sat in the chair, watching Mr. Ben in action. She couldn't help but admire his energy and determination. Suddenly, Mr. Ben took off to his apartment and asked the young men to give him a second.

"Summer... Summer!" Mr. Ben called out.

He was standing in his doorway, attempting to pull out a large cardboard box.

"What are you doing?"

Mr. Ben replied, "You cannot have this nice furniture with a small TV sitting on the floor. I'm gifting you this 55-inch television."

Summer quickly rejected his offer, "I can't accept this."

"I had it online to sell. I don't need it. My kids purchased it last year as a Father's Day gift. It's just been sitting in the box in a corner, taking up space."

"How much were you selling it for?"

"Give me $100."

Summer squinted at him, "I will give you $250, or you can push it back into your apartment."

Mr. Ben replied, "Deal!"

"Deal!" she repeated.

Summer was actually grateful that Mr. Ben showed up. Within an hour, he had put the delivery guys to work arranging furniture. He had a keen eye for design, and the room was transformed into a cozy living space. He even had them to mount her new TV above her fireplace. Thinking to herself how complete her apartment looked, "Now, I can invite Ebony over."

As the clock winded down, it was finally time for Summer to get dressed for the party. Dancing around the apartment and singing, she was finally dressed and ready to go. Adding her final wardrobe accessory - her pink bandana, was the perfect touch. But before she could leave, she had to call her Mimi. With such joy in Summer's voice, Miss Dangerfield encouraged her to go out and let her hair down. Summer had been so excited and caught up in her happiness and accomplishments that she had overlooked Miss Dangerfield's weak and shaky voice.

Summer dashed out the door, programmed Ebony's address in her GPS, and off she went. She couldn't arrive fast enough - tonight was the night that she'd shut Amber up. She said a little prayer that no one copied her outfit.

As Summer drove into Ebony's gated community, she marveled at the expensive homes. She drove slowly, as her eyes widened, amazed at what she was seeing.

She was suddenly startled by the GPS, which informed her that she was approaching her destination. As she approached Ebony's house, she noticed several cars lined up along the street. While attempting to parallel park, she was stopped in her tracks. The young lady who parked in front of her car had just exited her vehicle. The first thing Summer noticed was the young lady's left leg stepping out of her car with a black 6" faux fur stiletto heel. She was wearing a contrast lace asymmetrical sheer slip with a thong. Summer rubbed her eyes to make sure she was seeing right. She was frozen in shock, watching the woman's ass cheeks jiggle with each step. She immediately grabbed for her phone to call Ebony.

"Hello," Ebony answered,

"Ebony!" Summer yelled.

"Hey, Summer."

"A naked lady is walking up to your door."

Ebony giggled on the other line. "Get out of the car, crazy. It's a lingerie party."

Summer responded, "Wait. You told me it was a pajama party."

Ebony giggled. "Same thing."

"So, is everyone dressed like that?"

"Yes, pretty much."

"Goodnight. I'm going home," Summer said.

"No! Why?" Ebony protested.

"I have on pajama pants, Ebony"

"Me too. Come on. Just walk in; the door is unlocked."

Everything in Summer was screaming go home. Still, she exited her car, and with every step, she could hear her heart pounding in her ears.

As she pushed open the door, she was greeted by Ebony, who was wearing a sexy lace satin pajama pant set. All the other guests were dressed in the same manner.

Ebony took Summer by the hand and led her to her formal dining room. She could hear distant laughter from the other guests enjoying the party. There, Ebony took her to a table full of sex toys - none of which Summer had ever seen before. She introduces Summer to Michelle.

"Summer, this is Michelle. She is the host of my sex party. Girl, she helps you have better sex and a better orgasm."

Michelle handed Summer a gift bag and an order form, and then Ebony led her to the loudest area in the house. Summer's hands were sweating as she entered the main event area. Immediately, she noticed a presence in the corner of her eye coming down the stairs. It was none other than Amber.

Everything started to go in slow motion with every step Amber took. She was basically naked, wearing heart-shaped tassels, sequin nipple covers that covered only the areola, a short sheer lace slip, and thong.

As she reached the bottom of the steps, Amber loudly said to Summer, "What the hell are you wearing? Looking like Molly the Maid. You are so weird."

The entire room burst into laughter. Ebony gave Amber a shove in the back and then turned and addressed the crowd.

"Everyone, this is my supervisor, Summer."

Summer immediately found the closest seat, wishing she could just bury her face in a pillow. She was correct; she was a showstopper - she made everyone stop and laugh at her.

All the ladies were dressed sexy and confident in their skin. Summer felt so out of place. She wished the large crowd would just all move at one time so she could sneak out the door.

Ebony walked up and handed her a drink. Then, she sat hip to hip with her, so there was no quick getaway. Trying to relax, Summer took a big sip of the punch Ebony brought her. As she swallowed, the bitter, pungent taste hit her taste buds, and her throat immediately started to burn. Not wanting to make a scene and spit the alcoholic beverage out and possibly spray the other guest, she took a deep, hard swallow and eased the cup to the floor. She tried to avoid any facial expressions that would bring any more unwanted attention to her.

As the games began, the host walked around the room demonstrating sex gadgets. Summer wanted to curl up in a hole and die. As the ladies swapped stories on masturbation and techniques that they use to please their men, Summer felt like a fish out of water flopping on the ground, trying to find anything close to an environment that she could inhale and breathe in.

A new game began. This time, it was Truth or Dare. Summer could feel Amber's eyes burning a hole straight through her. Ebony had focused all her attention on Summer the entire night to make her feel comfortable.

As the game began, Amber yelled out, "Let my supervisor go first."

Unfamiliar with the game and afraid of what question Amber would attack her with, Summer chose Dare. She had to reach into the bowl and pull out a dare. Her paper read: Demonstrate deep throating using a cucumber.

Summer smiled and whispered to Ebony, "What do I have to do?"

Ebony said, "Suck on a cucumber."

Summer smiled. "Okay, that's stupid, but I can manage that dare."

"You have to be sexual with it, and don't vomit on my marble floors."

All the blood drained from Summer's face. "Come again."

"Just act like you're giving the best fellatio you have ever given."

Summer immediately dropped the piece of paper back into the bowl and said, "I don't want to play. I will sit this one out."

In typical Amber fashion, she immediately called her out in an angry tone.

Ebony chimed in, "Summer, just do it so that this bitch can shut up."

Summer looked up at Ebony and slightly shook her head no while whispering to Ebony, "I don't know how to do it."

Ebony gently grabbed her by the arm and scooted down to the edge of the sofa. She got closer to Summer to ensure she heard her correctly. Summer repeated, "I've never done it before."

Ebony immediately jumped up from the sofa and grabbed the cucumber. "I'm taking one for the team."

Amber quickly snatched the cucumber from Ebony. "No! Why can't she do it?"

With mumbles going through the crowd, Summer spoke up. "I have never done it before."

Amber asked, "Done what? Suck dick?" Summer dropped her head.

Amber got louder as she approached her. "Stop your lying. You have given head before."

She repeated herself repeatedly while arguing with Ebony as she attempted to defend Summer. Amber, with a sneaky grin on her face, blurted out, "I bet you're still a virgin."

There was a moment of horrified silence from Summer when she refused to answer.

Amber blurted out again with a burst of devilish laughter, "I'm right, ain't I? You're still a virgin. This explains everything. Molly the Maid hasn't let a man tap that ass yet."

The room burst out in laughter. Summer sprinted off the sofa and made a run for the door in tears. Ebony tried to stop her. She grabbed her from behind and made Summer stop and face her as they stepped outside the door. Seeing how visibly shaken Summer was, Ebony embraced her with a comforting hug.

"You have no reason to be embarrassed about being a virgin. That's a great thing to be proud of, but I will be honest with you. And this is not me condoning Amber's behavior. Hell, she's a bitch. She's been a bitch since I have known her."

Summer looked up and giggled as she wiped the tears from her eyes.

"Summer, you have to care about your appearance," Ebony said as she pulled on her pigtails. "This outfit would have been perfect for a 12-year-old slumber party," she added as she burst out into laughter.

Summer held her head up as she gave Ebony the side-eye. Ebony pulled her in for a hug.

"Don't look at me like that. Next weekend, it's me and you. We are going to get manicures and pedicures. What do you do to style your hair? Relaxer or flatiron?"

Summer replied, "Neither."

"Never?"

She shrugged her shoulders, shaking her head no.

Suddenly, the door swung open, and none other than Amber appeared. "Ebony, come on. You have a party to host; you are missing your party. The Virgin Mary has taken up enough of your time."

"She's right. You have guests to entertain. We will talk later," Summer said as she walked to her car.

She had the longest ride home ever. Flashes of tonight's events kept going through her mind as tears flowed down her cheeks. Embarrassed about her night, she wondered how she could ever tell Mimi about this experience. This would be listed as one of the top ten worst moments in her life. Not wanting to worry Miss Dangerfield, Summer vowed not to tell her about tonight's party. It was vital to her that Miss Dangerfield remained proud of her and didn't have to worry about her wellbeing.

When she returned to her apartment, Mr. Ben popped his head out to tell her goodnight. He could tell she had been crying. Never asking her what was wrong, he just held his arms out, gave her a big hug, and told her to say a prayer and start fresh in the morning.

As Summer undressed, she stood naked in front of the mirror, examining her body and comparing herself to the women at the party. She moved closer and closer to the mirror, gazing into her own eyes. Then, she spoke to herself. "Why do you let people run all over you? Why? Why?"

She suddenly dropped to her knees, curled up, and held her knees to her chest as she began rocking herself. Summer felt defeated and demoralized. She even imagined hiding in the parking lot and physically attacking Amber. She lay wondering how she could pull it off. She even thought maybe she could sic Mr. Ben on her. Her thoughts were interrupted when she heard a buzz from the other room. Her cellphone alerted her that she had a text message. It was a text from Ebony with a picture of Amber intoxicated and passed out with a dildo propped next to her mouth. Whipped cream was spread on the head of the dildo. Along with another picture of Ebony holding a can of Reddi-Wip with a message that read: "I will always have your back." At that moment, Summer felt she indeed had a friend.

# CHAPTER 4: Transformation

Monday morning was a doozy. Summer intentionally dragged around all morning, hitting the snooze button multiple times before finally dragging herself out of bed. She even stood in the mirror practicing her sick call-out voice. How could she face everyone? It was very noticeable that several of the ladies who attended Ebony's party Saturday night worked at the hospital.

Balling up on the sofa, she grabbed for the remote and noticed it was on the mantel next to the picture of her and Miss Dangerfield. She walked over to the mantel, picked up the photo, and ran her hands across Miss Dangerfield's face in the photo. She knew at that moment that she had to pull herself together, put on her big girl panties, go to work, and face the battle ax from hell, Amber.

***

The elevators opened, and as soon as she stepped onto the floor of the unit, she immediately locked eyes with Amber. It seemed like Amber had intentionally waited at the end of the nurse's station for Summer to exit the elevator. Instead of dropping her head and ignoring Amber, Summer looked directly at her with wide-open eyes. Summer had an icy stare, showing a lack of friendliness and no interest in Amber's antics this morning.

Amber's cocky expression quickly faded as she walked off, and she was very hesitant about having any conversation with Summer. Meanwhile, Summer, with her head held high and a determined stride, entered her office and closed the door. She had to prepare for a case conference with the nurses and was determined to set a demanding demeanor. No one would intimidate her or bring in unprofessional behavior without suffering the consequences.

Today's meeting was different. Summer stormed into the conference room with a stack of papers. Usually, she would let her charge nurse start the meeting. This time, Summer refused to take a seat. Instead, she stood at the head of the table, addressing her staff in a professional, autocratic supervisory demeanor. Summer started with the complaints on the unit, informing the nurses what would be tolerated and what wouldn't be. Amber immediately stuck her hand in the air, and before she could murmur a word, Summer stopped her in her tracks.

"All of my requirements are the requirements of this hospital's policies and procedures. So, I expect everyone to adhere to the hospital's policies. I'm not here to hold anyone's hand to ensure continuity of patient care is given at all times. I have printed out the employee handbook. When and if you read what we have discussed in this meeting and you have a question, it can be addressed one-on-one in my office."

Summer took her seat, turning the meeting over to her charge nurse. She sat with a blank stare, imagining herself jumping on the table and running towards

Amber, karate, kicking her in the throat. As the meeting adjourned, Ebony raised her hand and asked Summer if she could speak with her about the printed information she received. Summer instructed Ebony to remain in the conference room and told her that she would meet with her after everyone else left. As the last nurse exited the conference room, Ebony stood and closed the conference room door for privacy. Then, she turned swiftly and ran over to Summer.

"Oh my God! Where has this spicy individual been hiding? I'm so proud of you. Everybody's mouth was closed when you spoke this morning. I didn't think you had it in you. Amber asked me to go to lunch alone with her today. She said that she didn't want to be in your presence. She said you looked at her as if you were murdering her in your mind."

The room filled with laughter as they both burst into fits of giggles at the thought of Amber being intimidated by Summer. Ebony informed her that everything was set for this weekend. She requested Summer's presence at her home at 11:00 a.m. Saturday morning.

"I promise no dildos this time. And, please burn them plaid flannel pajamas," she joked.

HER TRANSFORMATION

The big day arrived, and Summer was clueless to what Ebony had in store for her. She rode in the passenger's seat, allowing Ebony full control of today's events.

When they arrived at their destination, Summer was once again in awe of her surroundings. Ebony had booked a day at a luxury spa. Summer was puzzled about why the receptionist handed her a robe after they signed in. However, Summer decided that she would just go along with no questions. Feeling apprehensive about a personal massage, she laid on the table with her stomach balled in knots. When the massage began, Summer tensed up with every touch. She wasn't too keen on the idea of lying on a table nude with only a thin sheet covering her. An hour had passed, and Summer was awoken after falling asleep during her massage.

Ebony snickered in the background and signaled for Summer to come along. "This is just the beginning," she said.

Next, they went for pedicures and manicures. After that, the most significant task of them all was tackling Summer's unattractive ponytail. Summer and Ebony ran around the hair salon like kids in a toy store. Summer chased Ebony as she picked out every neon color for the beautician to use to color Summer's hair. Finally, with a spin of the chair, her hair was transformed. The beautician kept it simple with a straight, long bob cut. It was long enough to pull it back into a ponytail if desired. Hesitant about the last task, Ebony's persuasive charm convinced her that a little bit of makeup never killed anyone. Summer finally caved to Ebony's suggestions.

Once the beautician had finished applying the last touch, Summer hesitated to open her eyes and see her final transformation.

Ebony gently touched her on the shoulder and said, "Beautiful." Summer slowly opened her eyes, and tears quickly formed as she was amazed by her new look. Ebony, being a jokester, grabbed her and hugged her.

"My little caterpillar has turned into a beautiful butterfly. Now, let's tackle those old maid clothes," she said as they laughed while walking out of the spa.

Ebony questioned her about her shopping habits and where she liked to shop. Summer informed her that Miss Dangerfield made most of her clothes and that she had been shopping at the local Walmart since relocating.

With a long eye roll, Ebony said, "To the mall, we go."

Summer felt like she was running a marathon. In and out, up and down, there wasn't one store that Ebony didn't visit. She spent most of the time hiding the price tags from Summer because anything over $19.99 made her hyperventilate.

Finally, that moment came when Ebony found the perfect dress. With great persuasion, she talked Summer into trying on a fitted dress that came an inch above her knees. Feeling out of her comfort zone, Summer couldn't deny that she looked drop-dead gorgeous in the dress. She agreed to purchase that dress, among other items that Ebony helped her pick out. Summer felt like her feet were blistered as they walked out of the mall with ten bags filled with clothing and shoes. It was after 6:00 p.m., and Ebony was planning the rest of their evening.

"I can't walk anymore," Summer blurted out. "I'm sorry... I just want to go home," she said, laughing and covering her face, knowing that Ebony was burning a hole through her skull with the death stare.

Ebony only agreed to drive her back to her car if she agreed to go out with her the following Saturday.

"I promise. I promise. Please take me to my car," Summer replied.

As the night winded down, Summer couldn't let it end without talking to Miss Dangerfield for two hours. She told her step-by-step about her eventful day. After the call ended, Summer strategically placed each new outfit in her closet. She organized her new shoes in order by color before taking a shower and relaxing. When she was done, she slipped on her new silk nightgown that Ebony insisted she purchased. She couldn't help but notice how sexy she felt when the silky material touched her skin. As she modeled in the mirror, she began to imagine what it would feel like to have a man desire her. Curious about intimacy, she replayed in her mind the stories the women told at the sex party.

She grabbed a cup of hot chocolate and her laptop. Snuggling up on the sofa, she searched for the word porn. Amazed at the number of websites that popped up, she began to click. Summer found herself watching a couple having sex. Feelings that she had never experienced before took over her body. She threw her head back and daydreamed that she was the woman in the video. As she imagined the guy kissing her between her legs, she could feel her nipples becoming erect. She took her hands and grazed them over her nipples, and she exhaled from the sense of euphoria. Butterflies fluttered in her stomach as she imagined the man kissing her stomach before slightly nibbling on her nipples as she grabbed his face to passionately kiss his lips.

When she opened her eyes, the man from her fantasy was none other than Mr. Ben. Summer jumped up and slammed the computer closed.

She immediately checked the bottom of her cup to ensure she had not slipped herself a mickey. She began dry heaving and holding her stomach as she walked to her bedroom. She quickly snatched the silk nightgown off and buried it in the drawer. She replaced it with a long cotton gown and then climbed into bed. She knew that she would have trouble sleeping because she was scorned from the image of Mr. Ben's face in her intimate thoughts.

# CHAPTER 5: She Found Love

As the stressful week came to an end, Summer avoided any confrontational encounters with Amber. She gave up lunch breaks with her only friend and settled for being alone at her desk, enjoying her sandwich without hearing Amber's voice—an even trade for her peace.

It was Friday afternoon. While sitting at her desk eating lunch, Summer received a text from Ebony asking to meet her in the cafeteria. Summer agreed, thinking Ebony would be eating alone because certainly, she wouldn't invite her to lunch with the troll. As she entered the cafeteria, she could see Ebony signaling for her to come to the table. Summer stopped and hesitated to take another step, her mind reeling at the unexpected guest at the table. Not only was she not alone, but three other individuals were sitting at the table - one being Amber, who stuck out like a sore thumb. Ebony rushed over and grabbed Summer by the arm, pleading with her to just come over to the table.

"I promise it will be fine. I wouldn't have invited you if I didn't think Amber would be on her best behavior."

Summer's eye roll, filled with disdain, was her only response to Ebony's plea as they walked towards the table before blurting out, "A wild barracuda can't be tamed."

Before Summer could take a seat, Amber's voice dripped with sarcasm, "Hello to you, Summer. It's clear that you have tugged at my best friend's heart.

"I'm still puzzled as to why she has taken such a liking to you, but I'm not here to fight anymore; I guess I will have to learn to share her. I don't have to like you, but we can be cordial with each other."

With her refusal to give Amber any feedback, Summer took her seat at the table and looked at Ebony with a head roll and pursed lips, making it evident that she intentionally kept her mouth shut to prevent her from saying what she felt. She had no intention of playing nice with Amber any longer, and the atmosphere crackled with the unspoken conflict.

Ebony, sensing the need to change the atmosphere, cleared her throat to get the ladies' attention. "We have to stop being petty," she said with her eyes fixed on Amber. "I have an exciting plan. I would love to take my friends out for a night on the town. Just friends and, I guess, frenemies enjoying drinks and dancing tomorrow night."

After a tense lunch meet-up, they made plans to meet at Ebony's house at 8 p.m. Ebony told Summer to come at 6 p.m., noting that she had some work to do. She had noticed that Summer had reverted back to her old habits of wearing a ponytail with no makeup. As they walked back to the unit, Summer and Ebony took the stairs, parting ways from the other group of ladies.

Ebony unable to hold it in any longer asked, "Why would you spend money on makeup and not attempt to wear it? Have you even taken it out of the box?"

Before Summer could reply, they arrived on the floor of their unit and noticed that Stevin was hanging around the nurse's station. His smile widened when he and Summer locked eyes. She walked by and smiled, "Hello, Stevin," she said, dropping her head as she walked to her office.

Summer was suddenly startled when Ebony pushed her way into her office and made her way to her desk.

"Are you really that oblivious, or do you just enjoy being alone? Clearly, you need a major boost of self-confidence."

"What have I done now?" Summer asked.

"I never knew Stevin existed until you started working here. He's been showing up on this unit several times a week for no reason or no clear reason in my book, looking like a lost puppy until he sees you. Hell, looking like the Joker…Yes, the Joker! He grins at you with that big Joker smile whenever you're in his presence. Typical Summer, you just ignore him like he isn't there."

"Stevin isn't interested in me. He has all you beautiful ladies to look at.

"Wait. Do you really think Stevin likes me?"

"Well, let's just find out. Come on; let's go to his office."

"No! I can't. What if you're wrong?"

"How would you know, Summer, if you never show interest in him? Now come on…"

"No, let's wait till Monday. I will get some new scrubs and let you put some makeup on me."

"Okay," Ebony agreed, "but I know one damn thing… I'm pretty sure you wear a medium scrub. Leave the damn 3X scrubs in the store."

Summer balled up a piece of paper and threw it at Ebony. "Get out of my office."

\*\*\*

Saturday arrived, and Summer suddenly had diarrhea and had to go to the restroom multiple times. She was a bundle of nerves as she tried to pick out an outfit six hours before she was due to be at Ebony's home.

Summer contemplated whether to cancel; she even typed the text as she stared at the send button. She couldn't cancel on Ebony after all she had done for her. Instead, she called Ebony and told her she had no idea how to prepare for tonight. In a calm voice, Ebony talked her through what to pack and what items to bring over. She suggested that Summer come over to her house since her husband was out of town, and she could spend the day at her home.

Summer was a nervous wreck as she made several trips back and forth from the car to the apartment. With every attempt she made to leave, she realized that she had forgotten an item that Ebony had asked her to bring.

Finally, she arrived at Ebony's home. They spent most of the evening trying on Ebony's lingerie and clothing. Surprisingly, Summer was eager to try on sexy clothing. With the possibility that a guy might be into her, she wanted to know how to present herself.

The time had arrived for them to get dressed. Ebony had laid out several outfits from her closet for Summer to try on, and Summer didn't object to any of them.

The clothes fit Summer perfectly, but she struggled to master walking in any of Ebony's 6-inch" heels.

With every step, she found herself face down on the floor. She even almost stumbled down the stairs in her multiple attempts to learn to runway walk in heels. Finally, they came upon a promising pair. Summer tried on a nude pair of 3-inch Louis Vuitton heels and actually conquered walking ten feet in them. Seeing the progression, Ebony proposed having Summer practice her catwalk by walking up and down her driveway. But just as she thought, she had found her rhythm. Six steps out the door, Summer stepped too close to the lawn, and down she tumbled. With every attempt to stand, she buried the heels deeper and deeper in the soil.

Poor Ebony was behind Summer, yelling, "You are ruining my Louis Vuitton heels." As Ebony helped her off the lawn, she shouted, "Your clumsy ass is wearing cheap wedges."

Summer had no problem with that. Going with the safer option, she got dressed in a pair of high-waist denim skinny jeans, a silver mosaic rhinestone halter top with a deep V-neck, and a pair of sequin wedges. However, she refused to come out of the bathroom. Ebony had to pick the bathroom lock and force her way in. Her mouth dropped when she saw Summer. She covered her mouth in awe.

"Baby girl, you are beautiful. If I were into women, hell, I'd bang you."

Summer pleaded with Ebony for another top. She couldn't dare walk out of the house without wearing a bra.

There she stood in a deep-cut V-neck handkerchief, as she called it. "There's no way possible I'm leaving out this door," Summer protested.

Ebony begged and pleaded for her to keep the entire outfit on until the other ladies arrived. Then, if she wasn't comfortable after that, she could change.

Ebony proceeded with Summer's hair and makeup, transforming her appearance. When she was done, Summer waited for the other ladies to arrive. She walked around and viewed Ebony's family photos. Summer kept her back turned away from the home's foyer when the doorbell rang. She stood in the living room, looking unrecognizable as the other ladies arrived. Monique and Sandra, the other two nurses who joined them for lunch on Friday, walked in with Amber.

They immediately asked, "Are we ready to go? When will Summer arrive?"

Ebony, with the biggest grin ever, called out to Summer. As she turned and walked towards the ladies, their anticipation of leaving turned into a surprise as they laid eyes on Summer's transformation. Monique and Sandra both flocked to her, flipping her hair and even slapping her ass.

"Why do you put all these hips under those big baggy clothing? You look so beautiful! I didn't even know it was you," they said.

Amber was immediately angered and didn't say a word. Summer wasn't used to Amber's mouth being shut. She felt so empowered that she decided not to change clothes after all. She decided to walk on the wild side. Anything that shut Amber up was good enough for her to wear out to the club.

As they pulled into the club parking lot, her stomach began to bubble. "How could I let Ebony talk me into this? I look like a sparkling high-class prostitute," she thought to herself. Her hands were sweating, and her legs trembled. She feared that her legs would become like jellyfish when she stood, and she would just flop to the ground.

Nevertheless, she trailed along like a little puppy as the other ladies high-stepped their way into the nightclub. All Summer could think was, "left, right, left, right, left, right." She was sounding off in her head to prevent herself from falling. As they entered the nightclub and turned the corner, Summer was suddenly blinded by all the flashing lights. The laser lights reflected off her mosaic rhinestone top, and she felt like she was lit up like a Christmas tree. She grabbed Ebony's hand and followed her to a table that Ebony had reserved. Once she reached her seat, she planned to stay glued to it all night. Amber immediately hit the dance floor.

Standing on stage next to the DJ booth was Christopher Diamond, a striking 6'2" tall, drop-dead gorgeous guy with grayish-brown eyes. He was a 25-year-old millionaire by inheritance.

You see, Christopher came from wealth. His parents were one of the wealthiest families in Beverly Hills, LA. Despite his privileged background, he aimed to present himself as a self-made millionaire and tried to distance himself from his father's grip while continuing to enjoy the perks of his high-powered connections. Christopher was part-owner of the nightclub and earned most of his money by renovating luxury homes in the LA area and renting out vacation mansions to the A-listers. He was known around town as a confirmed bachelor who had so much fun being single that he'd probably never settle for one woman, and he was perfectly okay with that. He was the youngest of three children and was known to be spoiled and self-entitled. Whenever he appeared anywhere, women flocked to him, including Amber.

As Summer walked through the club, he was drawn to her innocence. There was something about her that captured his attention. He knew the faces of every woman who walked through his club routinely, but he had never seen her before. He was familiar with Ebony since he had done business several times with her husband. He also knew Amber from being in his club weekly, throwing herself at him. However, it was something about Summer walking and clenching onto Ebony's arm for dear life that wouldn't let him take his eyes off her. Yes, she was nice-looking with a stunning body, but she didn't seem to belong. He was like a wolf sniffing out fresh meat as he made his way to Ebony's table.

He hugged her, asking, "Is everyone enjoying themselves?"

Summer kept her head down, making sure her sisters were still in her top. She didn't pay much attention to him. He reached across the table to shake her hand while introducing himself as the club owner. In her typical fashion, Summer shook his hand and dropped her head to take a sip of her Coca-Cola. The mere fact she showed him no interest only seemed to make him lock in on her harder. He walked around the table with a confident stride and gently placed his hand on her bare back, his touch sending a jolt of curiosity through her as he whispered softly in her ear.

"I have never seen you in my club before. Are you from around here?"

Summer looked up like a deer caught in headlights. She was speechless and thought, "No, this is not the time to be the mute imbecile." She straightened up in the chair, stumbling over her words; she cleared her throat, trying to maintain her composure despite her nervousness.

"No, this is my first time. I'm not from here."

Her legs trembled under the table as he leaned closer to her ear.

"Can I possibly get a dance before the night is over?"

Summer replied quickly with a snicker, "Oh no... You don't want to see me dance."

Ebony quickly interrupted the conversation and asked Summer to visit the ladies' room with her. Summer was too afraid to move and walk in Christopher's presence. However, she had no choice when he helped her up by pulling out her chair. Off she went with her left-right melody in her head. He stood and watched her walk away; he was more determined than ever that he had to have her. Meanwhile, Amber dashed over to the table as Christopher started to walk off.

"You're looking for me?" Amber asked.

He replied, "No, I got what I came for."

Amber gently grabbed his arm, demanding his attention. "I've been after you for years. When will my turn arrive?"

He smiled and proceeded to walk away.

"Besides, I saw you over there talking to Molly the Maid. She wouldn't know what to do with a real man like yourself. She is a virgin, and I'm all woman," she said, inching closer as her hand caressed his arm.

Amber didn't realize that she'd just set a fire off inside of him. He was even more determined to pursue Summer. Since losing his virginity at the age of fifteen to his twenty-five-year-old babysitter, all he knew was older, experienced women or younger women who only flocked to him because of his status.

While Amber sulked from yet another letdown from Christopher, Ebony and Summer stood in the mirror, touching up their makeup. Ebony noticed a mischievous grin on Summer's face.

Instead of expressing her actual concerns about Christopher, she said, "Wipe that silly grin off your face. He's way out of your league. You don't want to play games with that. Besides, we have to focus on getting you and Stevin on the same page on Monday. Hell, you need to send him a photo of you in this outfit tonight. He definitely wouldn't leave the 6th floor. I know you have his number. Give it to me, and I will send it," she said, snatching Summer's phone.

Summer quickly snatched her phone back with a playful pout, and they left the ladies' room, their laughter filling the air. As they returned to the table, the waitress was there, ready to take their drink orders.

Ebony ordered Summer a pineapple tequila sunrise and said, "You're getting tipsy tonight, and we're hitting the dance floor."

Summer had no objections; she secretly welcomed the alcoholic beverage. She wanted to get a buzz so she could loosen up, and if Christopher happened to return to the table, she'd be bold enough actually to have an adult conversation with him. Before she knew it, one drink turned into two. Summer spent most of the night daydreaming about Christopher's bold aroma of cologne and his soft, gentle touch on her back. She was mesmerized by the soft whisper in her ear and wanted to experience more of that rush. Before she knew it, Ebony was leading her to the dance floor. For the next couple of hours, they twirled each other around as she attempted to dance. It felt as though she and Ebony were the only two on the crowded dance floor. For the first time, Summer didn't care who stared or what she looked like. She was just having fun.

From a distant shadow, Christopher watched her the entire night. He couldn't take his eyes off her. They followed her every move. He was more than determined to make her his. He thought to himself that she'd be his white rose of purity. Her innocence drove him wild. What Amber meant for harm only enticed his thirst for her.

As the waitress cleared the glasses from the table, Ebony asked for her tab to close it out. She was informed that Mr. Diamond had taken care of the bill. Hearing this, Ebony quickly tried to usher Summer out of the club to avoid another encounter with Christopher, only to run right into him while they were exiting the club. Summer felt a tug at her arm. As she turned, she noticed him standing closely, as if he could just lean in and kiss her, a longing that seemed to consume her. She was frozen with such a deep desire to feel his lips touch hers.

Christopher asked if he could take her for breakfast and promised that he'd get her home safely. Ebony stood in the background quietly, as if she were afraid to voice her opinion in his presence. Summer politely declined the offer, her words laced with a hint of regret.

"I'm sorry, but I don't know you," she said.

Christopher stepped in closer. "Well, get to know me," he insisted, his determination palpable in his voice.

Summer placed her hand on his chest and pushed him back. She was afraid he'd knock her over if he got any closer.

"I'll take your number," she replied.

"No, I will take your "number," he countered.

"Do you have a pen?"

"No, I do not need a pen. Tell me your "number."

Summer verbally gave him the number without him writing it down or putting it in his phone. She left with an awkward walk, her attempt to appear confident betrayed by the slight tremble in her step.

When she reached the car, Amber looked as if she came straight out of the movie The Exorcist. Summer watched her the entire ride back to Ebony's home, wondering when her head would start spinning. The ride back was awkward. Nobody spoke, but Summer didn't mind because she had someone to daydream about, and it wasn't Mr. Ben. She tried to stop the image of Christopher kissing her all over, as she had seen in the porn video, but her mind couldn't stop thinking of his soft touch.

Despite Ebony's suggestion for her to stay over due to her drinking, Summer declined when she noticed Ebony's husband's vehicle in the driveway.

"I just want to get in my bed."

Summer was intoxicated - even more tipsy on Christopher. It was as if all of her senses had been awakened. On the drive home, she repeatedly checked her phone for his call, but there were no missed calls or texts. So, she showered and retired to bed, her phone nestled close to her ear, feeling the stirrings of love as she drifted off to sleep.

It felt like she had just closed her eyes when the jarring sounds of construction near the pool abruptly woke her. She realized that she had slept past noon for the first time in her life. Stretching with a sly grin, she felt a sense of accomplishment; she had finally managed to silence Amber. Her excitement rose as she searched for her phone, hoping for a message from the man of the night. But her smile quickly faded when she saw that the only person who had thought of her was Ebony, with a text: "Enjoyed you, Bae. Ready for our next adventure." Summer replied with a string of smiley faces. However, she couldn't help but feel disappointed about not hearing from the handsome mystery man.

Summer's mind wandered to her future with Christopher as she lay in bed. She envisioned the elegant wedding dress she would wear and the children they would raise, lost in a romantic reverie.

Suddenly, Summer remembered that she needed to call Miss Dangerfield to share last night's adventure. Miss Dangerfield answered with an awful cough and seemed short-winded.

"Mimi!" Summer yelled, "Are you sick? That cough sounds terrible. I'm coming home."

"Hush, my child," she replied. "I'm okay. You caught me having a choking spell."

"No, Mimi, that cough sounds really bad. Have you been to the doctor?"

Yes, I have, and they put me on some antibiotics and cough syrup. I should be ready to come out to visit you in a couple of weeks. I will let you know the dates to book the ticket."

Summer was filled with excitement at the news of Miss Dangerfield's possible visit, jumping around in bed and ignoring her medical intuition.

As she continued to talk about her night, Miss Dangerfield was quiet most of the conversation due to coughing spells when she attempted to speak. They ended the call on a happy note, making plans for their upcoming time together.

Unfortunately, due to construction, Summer couldn't get lost in the view of the pool. She spent most of her day checking her messages and restarting her phone to ensure it was working. She was disappointed when night fell, and there was no call or text from Christopher. She was convinced that he couldn't remember her number. Uncertain if she would ever hear from him again, she was already planning her next trip to the nightclub.

# CHAPTER 6: *Walking Into the Arms of Danger*

It was a dreary Monday morning, and Summer exited the elevator with her feet dragging.

"Good morning, Summer. Well, aren't you gloomy this morning," Ebony said, her voice laced with a hint of playful sarcasm.

Assuming that Summer's downward demeanor resulted from her inexperience with partying on Saturday night, Ebony could tell that Summer would rather be anywhere but at work. Summer was too embarrassed to admit that her somber behavior was due to Christopher not calling her. She kept replaying the night's events over and over in her head. Did she make a mistake when she turned him down for breakfast? The only way to be sure was to convince Ebony to take her back to the club on Saturday.

With a light tap on her office door, Ebony pushed her way into her office with her makeup bag in hand.

"Clearly, you have forgotten that we are on a mission today by the way you are dressed. I guess you never made it to the Scrub Outlet for new scrubs. Well, we will just have to work with what we have."

Summer was in no mood for a makeover. She pleaded with Ebony, "Not today. I just can't. Let's revisit this tomorrow."

"No, Summer. Why the change of heart? You were so hyped Friday about Stevin."

As she started to walk away, she stopped and turned, her gaze filled with genuine concern for Summer.

"Please don't tell me your change of heart had anything to do with Christopher."

The guilt was palpable in Summer's expression, which told it all.

"Listen, I didn't make a big deal of it Saturday, but Christopher is out of your league. He is a playboy and a conspicuous womanizer. You don't have the heart, knowledge, or skills to play his games."

"But, Ebony, I really liked him. He seemed interested in me. I was hoping we could go back to the club this Saturday," her mischievous smile adding an intriguing twist to her words as she looked up at Ebony.

Without a moment's hesitation, Ebony dismissed the idea. "Summer, as your friend, I'm telling you this for your own good. I would not steer you wrong. Christopher has a commanding personality and, might I add, a volatile temper. It's like throwing a kitten in a cage with a hungry lion; he'd devour you. Besides, let's not forget, has he even bothered to call you?"

Summer dropped her head and replied, "No."

"Well, GOOD!" Ebony said as she walked off, her words hanging in the air like a painful sting. She stopped and faced Summer, "Be prepared to allure Stevin tomorrow." Mocking Summer, she added, "He seemed interested in me. Hell, Stevin has been following you around like a lovesick puppy, but you fail to catch any of his vibes." With a roll of her eyes,

Ebony exited the office, leaving Summer to wrestle with her conflicting emotions.

Summer found herself unable to shake off the thoughts of Christopher, despite Ebony's warnings, not minding one bit at all if he devoured all of her. He had made her feel like she was the only woman in the club on Saturday night, igniting a sense of desire that was entirely new to her.

As she shut down her computer to prepare for lunch, Summer was drawn to the commotion outside her office. Amber was in a heated discussion trying to convince a flower delivery guy, who was carrying a bouquet of yellow roses, that he was headed in the wrong direction. However, Summer's name was engraved on the nameplate outside her office door, and the receptionist had already informed him of how to find Summer's office.

She stepped in and asked, "What seems to be the problem?"

"I'm looking for Summer Taylor."

"I am Ms. Taylor," she replied.

With an unsettling look, Amber returned to her seat at the nurses' station. Without a doubt, she knew who the roses were from. She was so mad at the idea that Christopher had chosen Summer over her that she sat silently, refusing lunch with the other nurses.

Summer placed the roses on her desk and removed the card before racing to the elevators to meet up with Ebony for lunch. Ebony remained quiet on the elevator; she also knew who the roses were from. In fact, she knew more than she was willing to say. She knew Christopher had made Summer his next target, and there would be nothing Ebony could do to pull her out of his trance. He got what he wanted when he wanted, by any means necessary, at any cost. Even if it meant stepping on whoever he had to step on to get it.

They walked in silence to the cafeteria. They decided to order from the hot bar. Ebony, with such despair on her face, turned to Summer.

"Friend, I love you. I have spoken my concerns, and with that, you are a grown woman. I don't want to take this moment from you because I know you are excited. Let me just say that you are walking up a road with no clear exit. This will also mean war with you and Amber, and I won't be able to tame her. She has been in love with Christopher since forever. No, he has never shown interest in her, but that hasn't stopped her from pursuing him. Now, with that being said, what does that damn card say?"

Laughter filled the table as Summer ripped open the small card that was attached to the roses.

"Hello, Ms. Taylor. It was such a pleasure to meet you Saturday night. The yellow roses express the way you made me feel. These beautiful sun-colored roses convey warmth, delight, gladness, friendship, and affection. Let's not forget good luck as well. Looking forward to seeing you again, Christopher" read Summer aloud.

"Hell, he forgot to mention that they symbolize jealousy. Did he write that on that damn card?" Ebony blurted out.

"Shut up, Ebony," Summer replied.

"He didn't call me. I assume he didn't remember my number. I never told him my full name. How do you think he knows my full name and where I work?"

Ebony dropped her head with a concerned look and hunched her shoulders, refusing to continue the conversation. It was clear that Ebony had her reason for being concerned. Instead of Summer questioning her about his past and what she knew, nothing would stop her chances of pursuing love.

Summer returned to her office, admiring her roses. As she took a big sniff of the roses, the smell of violets filled her nostrils. She spun around in her office chair; nothing could beat this day. Suddenly, her phone rang with an unknown number. She answered, clueless as to who was calling.

"Hello."

"Did you like your roses?"

Summer was speechless as she heard his deep, sexy, masculine voice.

"So, is that a, no?"

Still shell-shocked, she managed to say in a squeaky voice, "Yes! Yes, I loved them."

"So, you turned down my offer for a breakfast date. Can I get a yes to a dinner date?"

"Yes," she replied quickly, not taking any chance of losing contact with him again. "I mean… Yes, I'd love that."

With a slight chuckle, Christopher replied, "You won't make me wait until the weekend, will you?"

"No," Summer answered. "I am available after 5:00 p.m. during the week."

"So, will Wednesday at 7:00 p.m. work for you?" he asked.

"Yes, it will," she answered excitedly, her heart beating a little faster at the thought of their upcoming dinner date.

"Well, darling, I'm old school. I believe in picking up my date if that's okay with you. Text me your address, and I will see you Wednesday night. I will take care of all the arrangements," he said, his voice carrying such charm and a euphonous effect.

"Okay," I will," Summer replied, her voice betraying a hint of nervousness, her mind already racing with thoughts of their impending date.

Nearly falling out of her chair, she jumped up and ran out of her office to locate Ebony. She pulled her into the medical supply room while jumping around and silently screaming.

"I have a date with him on Wednesday! I have a date! Oh, Ebony, I'm so excited and scared at the same time. What will I wear?" Summer gushed, her eyes wide with anticipation.

"Oh, just put on one of those outfits Mimi made for you."

"No, Ebony, I might not get a second date."

"You see, we are both on the same page now," Ebony said with an unpleasant grin.

Summer walked off, visibly frustrated with Ebony's responses. She couldn't help but feel a pang of annoyance at Ebony's nonchalant attitude towards her date. Ebony could see the hurt in her eyes.

"Okay... Okay. Just put on a good pair of jeans and a nice blouse. I don't want you dressing up out of your comfort zone. Don't get me wrong, look nice, but be yourself. Don't go on this date with makeup on and nightclub clothing. He has to accept you for who you are. You are not from his surroundings, so don't try to be. Just be you."

Summer went home and spent the entire night thinking about her date and outfit. She even tried to reach Miss Dangerfield but didn't get an answer.

After much deliberation, she knew that Ebony was correct. She had to let him see her for who she really was. There was no way she could keep up the appearance she portrayed on Saturday.

The next day after work, she decided to return to the mall alone. She walked around looking at the mannequins and bought several outfits that were priced out of her comfort zone. She used the mannequins on the display as her muse and stopped trying to put the outfits together on her own. Summer felt comfortable in the clothes as she tried them on. She managed to put together simple yet sexy and casual outfits.

When she returned home and attempted to call Miss Dangerfield again, she finally answered after several attempts. The roles had reversed, and Summer was extremely upset as she chastised Mimi for thirty minutes before she let her speak. Miss Dangerfield just laughed at her attempt to reprimand her. She explained that her phone line was out due to a fallen tree, and she needed a new battery for her cell phone. Summer never questioned what she had told her. She immediately jumped to the next topic - Christopher. Miss Dangerfield was just as excited as she was and even gave her dating tips. While they talked, Summer informed her that she was sending her a package by mail.

"Don't keep sending me checks. I won't cash them, Miss Dangerfield said sternly.

Summer had made several attempts to send money back home, but Miss Dangerfield wouldn't accept it. Her concern was, would Summer be able to stand on her own two feet. Since Summer was rent-free, she wasn't convinced quite yet if she could make it on her own without any help.

## CHAPTER 7: The Date

Date night finally arrived. Summer's palms were sweating, and her legs trembled with nervousness. She couldn't even talk to Ebony, so she rejected her calls. She managed to pull off an outfit with stylish clean jeans, a well-fitting top, and a pair of flats that complimented her outfit. Her hairstyle was a mistake gone right. She had pinned her hair up to shower. After removing her silk scarf, she was left with a messy but cute pinned-up style. With a pair of diamond studs and a coat of mid-tone pink lip gloss, she was ready.

Suddenly, there was a knock on the door. When she opened it, there stood Christopher at 7:00 p.m. sharp. She could smell his cologne as the breeze hit her face. He was stunning, well-dressed, and nice-looking. All Summer could think was, "What did I do to deserve a date with him."

Christopher stepped into her apartment and embraced her with a hug. "We cannot leave without me telling you how beautiful you are. You are so well put together, and believe me - less is more," his words filled with genuine admiration.

Christopher took Summer by the hand and led her to his black Rolls Royce. Summer knew the car was beautiful and expensive based on its appearance, but she had no idea what type of car she was riding in or what its price value was. Christopher walked her to the car with his hand placed on her lower back. As

Summer reached to open the door, he grabbed her hand and stopped her.

"Please, do not do that," he said, his voice firm. Opening the door, he looked Summer into her eyes, stating, "When you are in my presence, you must let me be the man. Please never open your door or pull your chair out in my presence." His words carried a weight of control that was intriguing.

Christopher could sense her nervousness and tried to break the ice by asking where she was from.

"Nowhere special. I traveled here from the East Coast," she replied, her voice trembling slightly, praying she didn't have to talk about her childhood, only giving short responses. There wasn't anything Christopher didn't know about Summer, as he had already investigated beforehand, so some questions were only to see how transparent she'd be.

They arrived at an upscale steakhouse restaurant, and Summer wasn't familiar with this part of town. As they pulled into the restaurant's parking lot, Christopher drove to the entrance for valet parking. While waiting for service, Summer attempted to open the door to exit. Without speaking, he placed his hand on her leg to give her the gesture to remain seated.

"Sorry," Summer said, her eyes darting around nervously, unsure what to make of Christopher's impression of her.

When the valet opened Christopher's door, he walked around the car and opened Summer's door. As they walked into the restaurant, again Christopher placed his hand on her lower back. Summer waited for his cues, not wanting to make any more wrong moves. They were guided to their table, where Christopher pulled out her chair and helped her sit. Summer, feeling increasingly out of her comfort zone, scooted up and placed her elbows on the table.

Christopher leaned up and whispered, "Remove your elbows from the table."

She slowly placed her arms in her lap, thinking, "He hates me. I know this is my first and last date."

As the waiter filled their water glasses, Christopher spoke in French to order wine. The waiter returned and filled his and her wine glass.

"How do you like your steak," Christopher asked Summer.

"Well done," she replied.

He took the initiative and ordered for both of them. He ordered her a well-done steak with mashed potatoes and asparagus. Summer sat quietly and let him take the lead. He smiled at her.

"We will never get to know each other if you don't speak."

Summer was extremely nervous. When she tried to respond, she almost spilled her water glass. She dropped her head in her hands and apologized. Christopher found it amusing and let out a slight giggle at her innocent, shy behavior.

"What do you want from this date?" Christopher asked.

"I'd love to get to know you," she said. Feeling that if she didn't get out of her own way, this could very well be the last time she would see him. "Can I be honest?"

"Sure."

"I'm a nervous wreck," she said. "I don't want you to think I'm a weirdo."

"Now, why would I think that of you? I know you are nervous and shy. I just need to know what I can do to make you comfortable."

Summer surprisingly but boldly looked Christopher in his eyes and said, "I have never done this before."

"You have never been on a date?"

"I have never talked to a guy before."

"Never? Stop joking with me."

Summer immediately started to get flushed and dropped her head.

In a demanding voice, he said, "Hold your head up and look at me. You have never had any personal reaction with the opposite sex?"

"No."

"Well, dang. I really have to impress you. It's clear that no one has ever impressed you enough that you wanted to date them. Wow, I got a challenge tonight, so I don't have room for any mistakes."

At that moment, the ice was broken. Summer found herself spilling her entire life to him. She let him in on her most vulnerable thoughts. She didn't know why she couldn't stop talking. It was probably the mere fact that he hung onto every word she spoke instead of making funny faces or judging. The intensity and desire in his eyes as she spoke increased with every word.

After finishing dinner, they left the restaurant. Christopher suggested, "My house is less than ten minutes away if you would like to continue the night."

Summer felt a surge of conflicting emotions. She was torn between the fear of losing him and also not wanting to be misleading. She knew that if she declined, it might be their last date.

"That sounds lovely, but I have work in the morning."

Christopher didn't put up a fight. Instead, he drove her home and walked her to the door. Summer suggested he come inside to say goodnight because she had a nosey neighbor. They stepped in and closed the door, but she ensured they didn't go past the front door, a sign of her unease.

"I really enjoyed you tonight. Can we do this again?" Christopher asked, staring deep into her eyes.

"Yes, I would love that," she said, dropping her head and blushing.

"Summer, look me in my eyes," he said, gently touching her chin and lifting her head to force eye contact.

She obliged.

"Have you ever been kissed?"

She shook her head no, her innocence shining through.

"Can I kiss you if you are comfortable with it?" Christopher asked, his respect for her comfort evident in his tone.

Summer slowly nodded her head yes. With a tender touch, Christopher leaned in, his actions filled with a gentle hesitation, a desire for her to remember this moment. He placed a soft, lingering kiss on her pursed lips. As she felt his touch, she relaxed her lips, slightly parting them, and closed her eyes. He softly bit her bottom lip and whispered in her ear, "You are driving me mad."

He placed both hands around her head and kissed her passionately, pulling her face closer. His kiss was tender and full of warmth, with butterflies in her stomach, Summer could feel her nipples getting erect. She had a rush of lust that ran through her entire body. Her vagina had its own heartbeat. She stood in silence, savoring the moment. Christopher could feel her entire body give way to his touch. He pulled back with his hand still holding her head.

"Can I be your protector? Let me be that one consistent thing in your life."

Summer was still in awe, her eyes closed and absorbing in the moment. Christopher brushed his thumb over her lips and suddenly pulled back.

"Let me go; I don't want to take advantage of you."

In her mind, Summer agreed, "Yes, you're right." But her body was screaming, "Please take advantage of me."

Christopher sealed the night with a kiss on her forehead and departed, leaving Summer alone with her thoughts. She locked the door, leaned against it, and slid to the floor. "I'm in love," she thought. "I'm in love."

As she prepared for bed, she received a text from Christopher. His words, *"A beautiful ode to a white rose's purity, innocence, and youthfulness,"* struck a chord in Summer's heart. He ended the poem by calling her his white delicate rose. At that moment, Summer was sold; she knew he was her soulmate.

## DATING

Summer returned to work the following day, attempting to maintain her usual composure despite her elevated endorphins. She made an effort to remain professional and not to daydream about Christopher every second. While standing at the nurses' station, the elevator doors opened, and the same flower delivery guy appeared with two dozen white roses. She couldn't help but smile from ear to ear.

He recognized her and asked, "Do you want them on your desk?"

"Yes," she replied.

Amber was exiting a patient's room and crossed paths with him. They both gave each other a hostile look as they passed each other. Summer followed him into her office and gave him a tip for his service. Just then, Ebony burst into her office.

"You whore! You fucked him, didn't you? I can't believe you didn't tell me."

"No, I didn't!" Summer denied in a high-pitched voice.

"He tried? I know he tried," Ebony insisted.

"No, he didn't. It was not like that at all," Summer insisted.

"He didn't?" Ebony asked, her voice tinged with disbelief, with a shocked look on her face.

Cornered by Ebony for all the details, Summer walked her through her perfect night. Meanwhile, Stevin dropped by and noticed the roses. His demeanor changed instantly; his usual calm replaced by a sudden unease. He quickly exited her office, claiming to be looking for one of her floor nurses. Ebony pinched Summer.

"I told you he was into you."

However, Summer couldn't give Stevin a second thought. She was head over heels in love with Christopher.

Summer grew closer and closer to him as the days went by, feeling a deep connection that she had never experienced before. She spent every available second on the phone with him, cherishing every word he said. He even asked her to get a passport so she could travel with him. Miss Dangerfield was over the moon with excitement. Summer finally felt complete.

It was Saturday, and Christopher wanted to treat her to a special evening with a private chef at his home. He always made sure to pick her up so she wouldn't have to drive. As she waited for him this time, she was surprised by the knock at the door. Instead of Christopher, there stood a private driver. Mr. Ben stuck his head out the door but didn't have one word to say. He had obviously noticed Summer's new activity and became a little sore.

Despite the unexpected change, she was swept away like royalty and escorted to Christopher's home in style. After a lengthy drive, the driver informed her that she had arrived at Mr. Diamond's residence. Summer was grateful that she was alone in the car when she saw the mansion Christopher called home to take it all in. His luxury large mansion was located in one of the most beautiful districts in the city. As the car drove up the half-mile-long driveway, she was in awe of how breathtaking his home was. When the car came to a stop, she was greeted by Christopher.

"Where's your overnight bag?" he asked.

"We never discussed me staying all night."

"You stay almost an hour away. Why not just stay over?" his tone tinged with annoyance.

Summer could tell that he was visibly upset but trying to hold back. She walked up to the front door and entered the grand foyer, a sight to behold with its open wrought-iron staircase and marble columns. The beautiful, high-arched ceiling and sparkling windows added to the grandeur. Summer stood in the foyer with her mouth wide open in awe.

"You stay here alone?" she asked, her voice filled with disbelief at what her eyes were seeing.

He sarcastically replied, "Don't act like you didn't google me."

"I didn't," Summer replied, her tone changing.

She felt a little hostility from Christopher. "I could have driven. I really didn't think you would want me to stay over after only a week of talking."

"No, sweetie. You are correct. You are so correct," he replied, leading her to the washroom to clean up for dinner.

He had a private chef prepare a large, six-course meal for the two of them. After seeing his staff off, he returned to Summer.

"Let me apologize. I was here trying to prepare and make everything perfect. I want you to feel comfortable with me," he said, his voice carrying a hint of guilt.

Christopher insisted that she sit beside him, leaving no room for her to have any arm space. He stared into her eyes as they began with appetizers and said, "Take notes. I understand you're new at this, but this is how I expect to be treated as well," while seductively placing food in her mouth. For each course of the meal, Christopher remained close, feeding her and licking food off of her fingers. The slow tease with his warm, soft tongue caressing against her fingers as he sucked them sent chills throughout her body.

The entire meal was sexual, and Summer's heart was pounding as she was afraid that Christopher was expecting more than dinner.

After dinner, she stood at the sink, washing up, when Christopher walked up behind her and grabbed her, slightly lifting her off her feet. He asked if she was ready to go home or if she'd like to enjoy a movie with him.

Summer, feeling a mix of excitement and apprehension, agreed to watch a movie with him. As they snuggled up on the sofa halfway through the movie, Christopher was noticeably sleeping. However, Summer felt so uncomfortable. Nothing about his mansion screamed the comfort of a home. As badly as she wanted to be at her apartment, Summer was pretty sure she was staying all night. He seemed to feel her vibe as he popped his head up, rubbing his eyes, trying to stay awake.

"I will stay so you don't have to drive."

He reached over her to turn the projector screen off before taking her by the hand and leading her to the bedroom. Once in the bedroom, he handed her a T-shirt.

"I can sleep in my clothes."

"Jeans are not allowed in my bed," Christopher said in an authoritative voice.

Then, he led her to his large, immaculate bathroom to change out of her clothes. His bathroom and closet alone were the size of her entire apartment. Summer was nervous about coming out of the bathroom because she was basically naked. She only had on her underwear under the T-shirt.

While she stood in the mirror feeling self-conscious, Christopher knocked on the door, asking if he could come in. By then, she was at the washbasin cleaning her face. He placed a brand-new toothbrush on the countertop for her. She nervously watched him out of the corner of her eye as he began to undress right in front of her. He stripped down to his birthday suit. This caught Summer off guard; she had never seen a penis in person before. It was a shock to her eyes - and he was very well endowed. He started walking toward her, and she became nervous and dropped the toothbrush in the sink. Smiling with a mischievous grin, he picked up a pair of pajama pants from the counter and slid them on before walking out of the bathroom. Summer sighed in relief.

Finally, she made her way to the bed, the soft, luxurious sheets rubbed against her skin. As she eased herself into bed, he pulled her close to him and held her while he slept.

After a few moments of silence, Christopher asked, "Do you sleep with a bra on at home?"

"No," she replied.

"Well, why are you in my bed with one on now?"

She hesitated before sitting up to remove her bra. Summer couldn't get the image of his extra-large penis and exactly how it would fit inside her out of her head. When she laid back down, he pulled her close again and held her tight until they both fell asleep. She was later awakened by moans and Christopher thrusting around in his sleep. Summer was startled when he suddenly groped her between the legs and slid his hand in her underwear. As he rubbed her clitoris, she could feel herself becoming moist, trying not to respond to the pleasure; moans escaped her with every stroke of his finger. He removed his hand from her underwear, and she could hear him sucking on his fingers as he licked her juices from them. He rolled on top of her and began grabbing and sucking on her breasts. This was an indescribable pleasure that she never could have imagined.

Doubt immediately started to creep in. She was afraid of moving too fast, and suddenly, all of Ebony's warnings sounded off in her head.

She softly said, "Christopher, I'm not ready."

He immediately stopped, rolled over on his stomach, and then fell back asleep. Summer, a whirlwind of uncertainty, laid in the dark, wondering if her resistance would push him away. She finally drifted back to sleep and was awakened by Christopher at 6:00 a.m., informing her that he had business to handle and that he had a car ready to take her home. "Well, this is it," Summer thought as she headed to the bathroom to wash up and change back into her clothes. When she made it downstairs, he had breakfast, fruit and an English muffin waiting for her.

"I'm not hungry," she said, heading for the front door, her heart pounding with resentment.

Christopher called out to her, "Summer, come here. Is this how you want to end our night together? Kiss me," he demanded while picking her up, placing her on the countertop, and feeding her strawberries.

"Have you started the process of getting a passport?" he asked.

"Yes. I'm just waiting for it to come in the mail."

"Take off the last Friday of this month. And yeah, I won't hold it against you, but I need you to go get her waxed," he commanded, his tone leaving no room for a reply.

Summer was confused at first and then became extremely embarrassed; all the color drained from her face.

"Baby, stop being so shy. Just clean her up for Daddy. By the way, she tastes delicious."

As she walked away, he smacked her on her backside. Once she was in the car, she immediately texted Ebony to tell her about her hairy, embarrassing mistake.

Ebony responded: "You fucked him? You whore."

"Stop asking me that," Summer replied. "When it happens, you will know."

Ebony replied: "You're still a whore for letting him play between your legs. Hell, you might as well have given it to him if he can tell you what flavor your honey pot is."

After sending Ebony the middle finger emoji, she asked her to help her set up an appointment at the spa for a wax.

Over the next few weeks, Summer spent nearly every day with Christopher. Except for him filling her up in some weak moments, he kept his hands to himself. She knew he was playing nice because he had a big trip planned for her. As the weeks went by, she was set and ready to go. She and Ebony went over her checklist, and Ebony reminded her that she needed to freshen up with another wax before the trip. Summer replied that she didn't care if she looked like an African wild bush, she was never doing that again. They shared a hug and laughed at her experience.

## CHAPTER 8: Her Lost Innocence

Summer was nervous as she held Christopher's arm for dear life while the plane rolled backward away from the boarding ramp. Butterflies fluttered in her stomach, and she could feel every bump of the tires hitting the tarmac. As the plane picked up speed, she could hear clunking sounds and dug her nails into Christopher's arm. The more the plane accelerated, the more she felt a sinking sensation all over her body. She squeezed her eyes closed and prayed that they landed safely. She could feel the plane leveling off but was still afraid to open her eyes. Suddenly, she felt a soft peck on her cheek.

"Open your eyes," Christopher whispered his voice a soothing comfort in the midst of her fears.

She was spellbound as she slowly opened her eyes. Looking out the window, she could see the breathtaking blankets of fluffy white clouds below them, the sky a serene baby blue. The ground below had vanished, leaving her in a world of wonder. Christopher sat with a knowing smile on his face. He was aware that everything that she was experiencing was new. He took pleasure in knowing that he'd give her the first experience of everything.

Summer sat quietly; her mind was too clouded with fear to focus on what was expected of her when they arrived at the hotel.

As they flew over the Bahamas, Summer marveled at the turquoise blue water with green light wavelengths reflecting off the sandy ocean bottom. She could never have imagined experiencing anything like this growing up. She tried to hide her emotions as her eyes welled with tears. Christopher wiped the tears from the corner of her eyes.

"It's okay. It's beautiful. Isn't it?"

Summer didn't feel embarrassed by her emotions. There was something about Christopher that made her want to bare her soul. After a safe landing, she had no idea what to expect. She figured that they were headed to a nice hotel; however, they arrived at a luxurious ocean club estate in Casa DeLeon. There was too much to take in and no time to think. Christopher led her to the master suite, pulled a bag out of his suitcase, and revealed a seductive satin teddy.

Summer was instructed to shower and change; she knew what was about to happen; there was no denying it. He didn't fly her to paradise, just to hold her hand and walk on the beach.

Nervously, she walked out of the bedroom and located Christopher in the other room. He was standing at the large entrance of the villa that overlooked the ocean. Shirtless and sipping a glass of wine, he turned and noticed her standing in one spot with her arms wrapped around her body, attempting to conceal her breasts, which were visible in the satin teddy, that didn't leave anything to the imagination. He walked over as he poured her a glass of wine.

"Drink it; you'll need it," he said, startling her as he lifted her around the waist, her legs wrapped around his. Then, he seated her on the marble countertop, making her aware of its chill against her bare-naked bottom. Standing between her legs, he fed her strawberries and gently kissed her lips. He could feel her legs shaking nervously.

Looking into her eyes, he asked, "Do you trust me?"

While biting her bottom lip in an attempt to stop it from trembling, she nodded her head yes. He lifted her off the countertop, led her into the next room with a daybed overlooking the ocean, and laid her back gently. At that moment, Summer felt like she had lost all control. She was his submissive, and he'd do to her as he pleased. Christopher stared deep into her eyes, running his hand over her body as if he were studying her entire anatomy. He positioned himself on top of her and began to kiss her neck and slowly moved down to her breasts. He ran his warm, soft tongue slowly over her nipples as he gently blew on her moist nipples and nibbled on them. Summer felt her body craving for everything he had to offer. He used his teeth to slide the satin teddy up to reveal her bare vagina, planting small pecks between her thighs as if he were teasing her lady parts. As he worked his way back up, he took her arms and placed them above her head. He kissed her passionately as he held her arms in position.

He looked into her eyes, asking again, "Do you trust me?"

"Yes," she moaned.

"Well, cum for Daddy!!" he exclaimed as he spread her legs open and positioned himself to taste her. He placed her legs over his shoulders and ran his arms underneath them. He then grabbed onto her hands and interlocked their fingers together while holding her hands in position so that she could not move away from him. He wanted her to take everything he was giving. As he began to kiss her other set of lips, Summer threw her head back with her eyes rolling in the back of her head. She was immediately overtaken with a strong desire that she'd never experienced before. As he sucked and licked on her clitoris, her echo reflected throughout the large room as she screamed out in pleasure. Summer felt as if she was on a rollercoaster of pleasure. She could feel her stomach tighten up with intense butterflies as if she was being sucked to the edge of a ledge; when she finally reached the drop-off, she suddenly dived into an intense pleasure of climax.

Christopher held her hand tightly and sucked harder. She curled her body up, squeezing his head between her thighs, feeling as if she couldn't take anymore. He sucked her clitoris harder and harder; She was now back on the drop-off of pleasure as she experienced her second orgasm. He could feel her legs shaking, knowing he had her right where he wanted her. He released her hands and leaned in with a passionate kiss. As she lay panting and breathing heavily with her body shaking, he pulled the teddy over her head and left her lying in complete nudity.

Then, he stood up with his erect penis in full exposure. Summer's eyes bucked. His penis was massive – even bigger than she remembered.

As he stood and rolled the condom onto his erection, her entire body shook with nervousness. He crawled between her legs and demanded her to relax as he pulled her body into his. She could feel his giant cock as he guided it inside with no hands. Anxiety built as his large throbbing manhood attempted to penetrate her for the first time. He was cautious and moved slowly, but she could still feel an enormous amount of pain and burning. She tried squirming her way from under him. However, he kept repeating, "You have to relax."

She replied, "It hurts, Christopher."

He slid his head between her legs and used his tongue to lubricate her tight opening. Then, he sat up on his knees and pulled her bottom close to him, raising her hips. He told her to hold her legs apart, exposing her plump juicy cherry that he was so eager to pop, watching himself guide his pulsating cock in and out of her, trying to loosen her up. Summer tried to relax, but she was still in great discomfort. She turned her face with teary eyes as Christopher stared into them as he could see through her soul. Finally, he felt a pop. Knowing that he had stretched open her hymen, he slid all of himself inside of her inch by inch.

Composing himself, he denied the urge to pound deep and hard, slowing his strokes as he forcefully kissed her. He could feel her body relaxing as he gently stroked in and out. With each moan that escaped her, his strokes became more intense, pounding deep into her muscles. Just as Summer felt her muscles giving in to the pleasure of his throbbing cock, she felt him getting harder and bigger as if it were growing inside of her. He began to pound harder and faster. Suddenly, with one deep thrust, his body locked up with intensity as he shouted her name. His body began to jerk, and Summer could feel his cock throbbing inside her as electric jolts of pleasure consumed him. He rolled over, collapsing next to her; as their eyes met, he grabbed her by the head and kissed her forehead.

"You're mine now. Damn, my pussy is good," he proclaimed as he tried to catch his breath.

Summer, unsure what to do next, waited for Christopher to leave the room to refill his wine glass before she headed to the bathroom for a shower. Closing her eyes, she let the warm water hit her face. As the water ran down her naked body, flashes of moments of her first time went through her mind. She couldn't imagine that being with Christopher would feel this great. She was suddenly startled out of deep thought as Christopher joined her in the shower, asking if she was okay. When he attempted to wash her body, she became stiffer than a rock, and all of her muscles tensed up. She used her arms to cover herself. He grabbed her arms and demanded that she hold them in the air.

"You are beautiful," he said as he began to wash her body. He gently grabbed her by the face when she dropped her head, avoiding eye contact. "Never hide your body from me. You are not allowed to cover yourself up in intimate moments. You're taking away from my pleasure."

With a rough but sexy hair pull, he forcefully kissed her, sliding his hand down her back, and with a swift lift, his hands cradling her bottom and the backs of her thighs. She wrapped her arms around his neck and shoulders as they passionately kissed while the lukewarm water ran down their bodies. He placed her back against the tile wall of the shower and slightly lifted her as he slid every inch of himself in her. He fit like a perfect glove, bouncing her up and down with his muscular, solid arms. Summer knew Christopher was the one; at that moment, she was his. They would spend the rest of the vacation having hot, passionate sex; Christopher sexually molded her to fit every idea he thought she should be. Summer no longer needed to stare at the 16'x 32' swimming pool in her apartment complex and imagine that it was the ocean; she was finally in paradise.

# CHAPTER 9: FROM PARADISE TO HELL

It was time to return to reality, and Summer didn't mind one bit because she was boarding the airplane and returning home with Christopher. As long as he was by her side, nothing else mattered. She was so lost in her thoughts that take-off was a breeze. She closed her eyes and reminisced on the past forty-eight hours. She could still feel the sand between her toes as the warm ocean water splashed against her skin and the comforting warmth of the sun on her face. She could feel Christopher carrying her into the ocean on his back and holding her as she closed her eyes and floated so blissfully on her back. He held her tight as he waved her around in the water while leaning in and kissing her lips so gently.

Christopher tenderly caressed Summer's leg as she slept when the plane landed.

"Wake up, baby. I must have really worn you out this weekend. You've slept through the entire flight. I had to elbow you a couple of times because the other passengers started complaining about your snoring. The stewardess wanted to kick you out of first class," he teased, a mischievous glint in his eyes.

"I was snoring?" Summer asked, feeling embarrassed.

Christopher couldn't keep a straight face as he burst out in laughter. "No, sweetheart. You sleeping so peacefully just means I did my job," he said, smiling with confidence as they exited the plane.

While waiting at the baggage claim, Summer noticed everyone around her talking on their cell phones. At that moment, she realized that she needed to check her messages. Christopher had asked one thing of her on this trip, and that was to give him all of her attention. He requested that she turn her cell phone off until they returned home back to the States. Summer silenced her phone and kept it in her purse without checking it once. She was so caught up in lust and luxury that she had forgotten entirely about her cell phone. She rumbled through her purse for her phone; her heart skipped when she noticed several missed calls and texts.

Several of the missed calls were from her old job back home and urgent text messages from Ebony. A wave of dread washed over her as she anticipated receiving news she wasn't prepared for. Summer's first thought was Mimi, and she frantically dialed Miss Dangerfield's number.

When a male voice answered, "Hello."

"Mr. Jefferey! Mr. Jefferey, is that you?" Summer's voice was urgent, filled with the need for answers.

Mr. Jefferey was a close friend of Miss Dangerfield. Summer always felt they were bed buddies, but Miss Dangerfield would never admit it.

"Why are you answering Mimi's phone?" Summer asked.

"Summer, my child, I'm sorry. I don't know how to tell you this."

Before Mr. Jeffrey could tell her that Miss Dangerfield had passed away, Summer was struck with a sudden shock. She dropped her phone, overcome with emotion.

"No, no, no," she repeated as she backed away from Christopher. Unaware of what was happening, he picked up Summer's cell phone.

"Hello, this is Christopher Diamond, Summer's friend. May I ask who I am speaking with?"

Mr. Jeffery, a long-time family friend, explained that he is a very close friend of Miss Dangerfield and informed him that she had passed away. He also said that they had been trying to reach Summer for the last two days. Christopher looked at Summer, who was standing in disbelief. She waited for Christopher to say that Mimi was sick, but she was okay. He took her by the hand and led her into the VIP lounge at the airport.

"Is she okay? Is she okay?" Summer repeated.

He enveloped her in a hug, his voice filled with empathy as he softly said, "She's gone, baby. Your mother is gone."

Summer's legs suddenly gave away as she fell into Christopher's arms. She knew the feeling of loneliness, sadness, and being afraid, but she had never experienced heartbreak like this. She felt like a strong force of wind had knocked the breath out of her. As she panted and sobbed, Christopher held her tight and promised not to leave her side. Her cell phone rang; it was Ebony calling.

Summer was in distress and unable to speak. Christopher, understanding her emotional state, asked Ebony to inform her employer of the news. He assured her that he would assist with getting Summer back home. Christopher made several calls to book a red-eye flight to New York for him and Summer. Heartbroken and still in disbelief, Summer would find comfort in Christopher's arms as she wept the entire flight back to her hometown.

Christopher, determined to be supportive, had reserved a car service and booked them a hotel. He insisted that Summer rested before going to the hospital. However, Summer was listed as next of kin and needed to sign to release Miss Dangerfield's body to the funeral home. She had requested to be cremated. Summer couldn't rest until she saw her, so she insisted that they go straight to the hospital.

Christopher arranged for Mr. Jeffery to meet them at the hospital. He drew the line when it came to seeing a dead body. Sadly, Summer had to be sedated after arriving at the hospital. Seeing Miss Dangerfield's lifeless body was too much for her to handle. She had to be dragged away as she clenched onto her cold, stiff corpse, begging her to open her eyes.

The following morning, they met Mr. Jeffery at Miss Dangerfield's home. Summer walked around, smelling and touching all of Miss Dangerfield's belongings, and noticed that she had several prescription bottles at her bedside, two of which were target therapy medications that treated cancer. Summer had been so distraught about the news of her passing that she never learned the cause.

Mr. Jeffery informed her that Miss Dangerfield had been diagnosed with Stage IV breast cancer a month after she relocated. Not wanting to jeopardize any chances of her succeeding with all her new opportunities, despite the daunting news, Miss Dangerfield thought it'd be best to battle the cancer on her own and not let it overshadow Summer's opportunity. Knowing Summer would give it all up to be by her side. She never lost hope that she could beat it - even when doctors informed her that it was terminal.

"Please don't be angry, Summer." Mr. Jeffrey pleaded. Her happiest days were hearing how you were adjusting and doing so well... Summer, I truly hate to deliver another blow, but I have more bad news. The bank wants to foreclose on her home.

"Why? How? This home is paid for."

Mr. Jeffrey explained that Miss Dangerfield defaulted on a second mortgage loan. She took out the loan to pay for Summer's car so she could have transportation to relocate. With her sudden illness, she got three months behind on the loan payments.

"Why would she do that?" Summer cried out. "I sent her money, and she would not accept it. I have to save her home. I can't let her lose her home because of me."

Christopher spoke in an aggressive tone. "Summer, this is no longer your home. You live in another state. Why would you put money in this house, and it's falling apart? When will you have the time to put in the work that it needs? You don't need the added stress."

Christopher could see Mr. Jeffery's facial expression after the tone he took with Summer, so he excused himself to the restroom.

Mr. Jeffery asked Summer, "What do you know about this young fella? Are you sure he is a good character?"

"Yes, Mr. Jeffery, he is the best."

Christopher was eavesdropping from the other room and became very angry at Mr. Jeffery for questioning his character. When he returned from the restroom, he walked right past Mr. Jeffery without acknowledging him and told Summer that he would be in the car waiting for her. She was overwhelmed with grief and unable to tend to Christopher's ego. She asked Mr. Jeffery if he would meet her at the bank first thing in the morning to inquire about catching up on the payments on Mimi's home. She didn't want Christopher to know her plans, so she kept it to herself. Summer wasn't willing to listen to anyone telling her to let Miss Dangerfield's home be taken by the bank. This would always be her home.

### Saving Her Home

The next morning at 7 am, Summer eased out of bed, leaving Christopher asleep while she snuck out to meet Mr. Jeffery at the bank. She took a cab, praying she could get everything sorted out before their flight. While at the bank, she was surprised to learn that she would inherit Miss Dangerfield's home once the second mortgage was paid off.

Due to Miss Dangerfield's sudden passing, the bank was willing to allow Summer to get the loan in good standing. Upon paying off the loan, the deed would automatically be transferred to her name.

During the meeting, Summer received several calls and texts from Christopher. As she didn't want the backlash from him, she chose to keep the details of the home to herself. Summer requested that Mr. Jeffery stay in the house rent-free, and she would send whatever money that was needed to do repairs. She was determined to bring Mimi's ashes back to her home, where she belonged. Looking at her watch, she realized that she had no time to spare as her flight was leaving in an hour. She called Christopher and explained that she was packing up at Miss Dangerfield's home and had lost track of time. She apologized for missing his calls and texts due to her phone's low ringer. From Christopher's voice, she could tell that he was upset.

When she arrived at the hotel, she had just enough time to grab her suitcase and go. As she entered their hotel room, Christopher was furious, his voice filled with anger and urgency, and he yelled, "We are about to miss our flight! I haven't even called for a car."

While grabbing her suitcase, Summer explained to him that Mr. Jeffery was downstairs and would be taking them to the airport. Too angry to address her, he pushed past her and headed to the elevators. As they walked out of the hotel, Christopher paused and pulled her by the arm.

"I know damn well you don't expect me to ride in that."

Mr. Jeffery was waiting for them in his 1989 white Ford pickup truck with junk in the truck bed he was hauling to the dumpster.

"Baby, please," Summer pleaded. "We will miss our flight."

With great hesitation, he climbed into the truck, having to put his Gucci luggage on top of the trash. The smell of oil hit him with full force, but Christopher didn't speak a word. When they arrived at the airport, he quickly jumped out of the truck, leaving Summer behind. Mr. Jeffery looked on with great concern.

To their surprise, they learned that their flight had been delayed, so Christopher led Summer into a private living room within the lounge of the VIP area.

As soon as they were alone, he aggressively snatched her by the arm.

"Don't ever pull that shit with me again!"

"Christopher, you're hurting my arm. Please let me go," she pleaded, her voice trembling with concern.

As she attempted to pull back, his grip got tighter.

He bellowed, "Is it okay to sneak off in the middle of the morning and leave me in a strange city without one word? I would have never thought you'd be so damn reckless. I am Christopher Diamond, and you have me picked up at a five-star hotel in a damn beat-up truck. Clearly, you are not the one for me. Answer me, dammit!" he roared as he yanked her by the arm, his face contorted with rage.

Tears flowed down her face as she answered in a soft, squeaky voice, "I'm sorry."

He released her and ordered her not to speak to him for the rest of the trip. Then, he walked away, leaving Summer at a loss. She slowly took a seat with a stunned look on her face. She had just been dealt a second blow to her heart. In the span of two days, she had lost the two people who brought the most joy to her heart. She was visibly upset, her tears flowing freely. She asked herself, "What just happened?" as she put on her shades to hide her eyes. She let her hair down from its ponytail, using it to cover as much of her face as possible.

Finally, they boarded the plane. However, there was no eye contact from him as she sat next to him on the flight. Summer was so emotionally drained and upset that she couldn't stop her tears from flowing.

When they arrived at Abraham Lincoln Capital Airport, Summer, feeling utterly alone, slowly walked behind him as they departed the airport. She assumed she would have to find her own way home, so she sat on the bench outside the terminal as Christopher was greeted by his driver. Still very irritated with Summer, he looked back at her, sitting with her head down and looking hopeless. Feeling a sense of guilt, Christopher called out to her and requested that the driver take her bags. Then, he grabbed her by the hand and escorted her to the car.

They remained silent throughout the car ride. When they arrived at Christopher's mansion, Summer assumed that he had the driver to drop him off first because his home was closer. She remained in the car as he got out. When he noticed that she wasn't exiting behind him, he reached in and pulled her by the hand. She was confused but didn't question him; she simply followed Christopher into his home. After the driver put down their bags, Christopher locked the door behind him. Summer stood in the foyer looking like a lost puppy; he took her by the hand and led her upstairs. She willingly followed him to the bathroom. Christopher turned on the shower and then turned to face Summer. He looked into her exhausted face, her eyes heavy with fatigue and swollen from crying and lack of sleep.

He helped her undress and step out of her clothes. Summer stepped into the shower, feeling defeated as the warm water cascaded over her, soothing her troubled soul. With her eyes closed, she stood under the showerhead, letting the water run down her body, wishing she could wash the past two days down the drain. She could feel Christopher's presence as he stepped into the shower and joined her. When she opened her eyes, he stepped before her and pulled her to him. She leaned in, placing her head on his chest. He ran his hand through her wet hair and caressed her neck.

"I'm sorry. I'm so sorry," she cried out.

With a gentle chin lift, he looked into her eyes and said, "No, baby. I'm sorry. Seeing you in that state of mind and waking up without you next to me frightened me. I admit I didn't handle it right, but I couldn't handle the thought of something happening to the woman I am falling head over heels in love with. I'm sorry, baby. Please don't let today's events cloud your judgment about us," he pleaded, his love and sorrow for her shining in his eyes.

Nothing mattered but Christopher at that moment. Summer just wanted one out of the two heartbreaks to stop.

Kissing her softly, he turned her around as he washed her back. She could feel his body next to her bare-naked skin as he reached around her and ran the washcloth up her thigh and then between her legs. He dropped the washcloth and used his fingers to massage her clit. Kissing her neck, he runs his tongue down her back. Chills ran through her body as he gently bit her butt cheeks while sliding his fingers inside her, feeling her inner moist as he took pleasure in feeling her muscle grip his fingers with each stroke. He turned her around, picked her up, and stepped out of the shower with their bodies dripping wet.

Christopher sat Summer on the edge of the bed as he dropped to his knees in front of her, taking his fingers and slowly sliding them in and out of her. He gazed deep into her eyes as he placed his fingers full of her wetness in her mouth, enjoying the sucking sensation as she tasted her own juices. With a swift pull of her legs, bringing her throbbing essence closer to taste her, she gasped at his sudden movement. He placed sensual small kisses on her clitoral hood before sliding his tongue along her slit; he flicked his tongue over her clit and sucked until she flooded his mouth with her sweet juices.

Summer had her hand on the back of his head, submerging his face in her moisture as she got wetter and wetter. She moaned and called out his name, begging for him not to stop. Pushing her back onto the bed, he savored each second as he slid his large pulsating cock in her inch by inch while passionately kissing her with each stroke. He flips her over on her stomach while pinning her arms behind her back as he enters her from behind. Sliding his hands up her neck, he twists her hair around his fingers and, with a slight jerk, causes her to arch her back, keeping her in the position with a rough hair pull.

He pulls her against him, caressing her breast as he strokes deeper and harder until electric jolts of pleasure consume them both until they collapse from exhaustion. At that moment, Summer knew that her heart was heavy, but Christopher, making passionate love to her was the medicine she needed. She found comfort in his arms as he held her tightly throughout the night.

# CHAPTER 10: HER NEW REALITY

Summer spent the next two weeks at Christopher's home, finding peace in his presence. During this time, she shut herself off from the outside world. When she finally turned her cell phone on, she saw that she had received several threatening but hilarious texts from Ebony. She replied that she would return to work the next day. Although she felt like she could lay on his sofa for eternity, Summer knew she had to return to reality. While packing her bags, she called Christopher to inform him that she would be returning home and back to work. He tried to persuade her to take some more time to grieve and remain at his home. However, he had an out-of-state business trip, and Summer was afraid to stay in his large home alone.

When Summer arrived home, she was bum-rushed by Mr. Ben before she could enter her apartment.

"Now, baby girl, what the hell! I haven't seen you in weeks."

She informed him that her mom had died, and he gave his condolences and let her grieve in peace.

Summer found solace in knowing that Miss Dangerfield was home. Mr. Jeffery had taken care of picking up her ashes, burying the urn in her yard, and planting a memorial tree in her name.

As Summer thought about how much she'd miss her mom, she prepared herself for work. She knew that she would be two weeks behind in paperwork, so she planned to use the weekend to catch up. When she pulled into the parking lot at work, she knew that the day wasn't going to be easy. She had no desire to talk about her loss.

As she dreaded the elevator doors opening to the unit, she walked off the elevator to find cards, balloons, and flowers. The staff had gone above and beyond to express their sympathy; even Amber had signed a card. Stevin was standing by her office door. He embraced her with a hug of sympathy. Ebony gave her an hour alone in her office before barging in.

"Look, Bitch. I know you're still hurting, and yes, I understand. But I'm not going to ignore the fact that you're walking with a new gap that you didn't leave here with."

Summer burst out into laughter. Leave it to Ebony to put a smile on her face. She shared her most intimate details, not leaving one detail out.

"You see, Ebony, he's good; he really is good to me."

The day went much better than Summer anticipated. As the day came to a close, she gathered all the work she had missed and took it home with her for the weekend.

When Christopher returned to town, he made several attempts to get Summer out of her apartment. However, she was buried in two weeks of work and needed the alone time to catch up. She knew being in his presence would mean spending more time on her back and getting no work done.

Ebony also kept pressuring her to get out and enjoy herself, but she had turned down every attempt. She had finally convinced Christopher to accept that she was staying home for the weekend. Now, Ebony was riding her. Suddenly, there was a knock on the door. Through the peephole, she saw Ebony dressed sexy and ready for a night out in town.

Ebony convinced Summer that she could visit Christopher at his club and kill two birds with one stone.

"You can party with me and then go home with him and let him blow your back out."

Summer had no choice because Ebony wasn't bending. She put together a nice outfit, and off they went. Summer decided to surprise Christopher when she arrived at the club, so there was no communication with him before they arrived. Ebony had not reserved a table, so there was only standing room available. They walked to the bar to order drinks. Moments later, Ebony was pulled to the dance floor. Summer sent Christopher a text to inform him that she was there at his club and that Ebony had convinced her to come out. After receiving no reply, she attempted to walk around the nightclub and locate him. Her phone buzzed, and she'd finally received a reply from Christopher asking her to meet him at the exit door at the back of the club.

She spotted him standing down the hallway and quickly made her way to him. As she leaned in to kiss him, she could smell the alcohol on his breath. He turned his face to avoid her kiss and snatched her by the arm, dragging her out of the club. She tried to snatch away, but he only became more aggressive, grabbing her arm with a bone-crushing grip.

He shouted, "You haven't spent an entire week with me, but you can come clubbing!"

As he pulled her to his car, he walked faster and faster. Summer lost her footing and fell to the ground. He helped her up, but he was still handling her with such aggression as he forcefully put her in his car. Meanwhile, Summer yelled, "I came out to be with you, Christopher! I came to spend time with you."

In a loud, angry voice, he screamed, "How the hell did you come to a nightclub to spend quality time with me? You are in a fucking relationship! Are you a whore?"

Summer didn't answer; she just rolled her eyes.

"I asked you, are you a damn whore? No, you're not. That is not a good look for you nor me."

Feeling angry and very upset, Summer attempted to text Ebony to let her know she had left the nightclub. However, Christopher reached over and slapped her phone to the car's floorboard. With a surprised look, she attempted to pick her phone up.

This time Christopher screamed, "Leave it, dammit! You have disrespected me, but Ebony's feelings are what you are concerned about. Fuck this! I don't want you in my presence." He quickly did a U-turn in the middle of the street and dropped her off at her apartment.

"Christopher, please," Summer pleaded.

Christopher remained silent, staring straight ahead without acknowledging her. Before she could close the door properly, he sped off, leaving skid marks on the road. Summer was confused and hurt as she made several attempts to reach Christopher throughout the night with no response. She was too embarrassed to tell Ebony the truth, so she sent a text and informed her that she was home. The following day, Summer called Ebony and told her the entire truth. Surprisingly, Ebony took Christopher's side and convinced her to look at it from his point of view.

"He had been out of town. Then, he came home with no real embrace. You refused to see him. Hell, he was probably feeling sex-deprived," she said, giggling. "You know men do dumb shit when you withhold the good-good. Oh, I forgot! You don't know," she added as she burst into laughter.

"So, bitch! What you are saying is that this is your fault, and you're going to help me get back in his good grace."

"Oh, girl, just give him some good head," Ebony replied.

Summer paused for a moment. Ebony burst out in laughter again.

"Oh, I forgot you don't know how to do that either. My poor friend is up the creek without a paddle."

Ebony instructed Summer to text Christopher, asking to meet up tonight at 6:00 p.m.

Christopher replied that he wouldn't be home until after 7:00 p.m. but that she knew the codes to his home. So, she should just be there when he arrives. Summer relayed the message to Ebony.

"Great," Ebony said. "I will see you in an hour."

She unexpectedly hung up, leaving Summer still holding the phone. "Hello? Hello?"

An hour later, Ebony showed up at the door with bags of dildos, bananas, and cucumbers.

"Why do I need a banana and cucumber," Summer asked.

Ebony peeled the banana and told Summer to delicately suck on it. Summer, being silly and not taking it seriously, stuffs the banana too far in her mouth and chokes. She bit down on the banana and started chewing.

"Bitch you just answered your own question. First lesson of what not to do," Ebony said, snatching the half-bitten fruit and discarding it. "Now, let's start from the top."

Summer spent the next three hours learning the techniques of a blow job and twerking moves for the bedroom. With sexy lingerie and lockjaw, off she went.

*Sink Or Swim*

Summer stood nervously in Christopher's kitchen. If Mimi hadn't taught her anything else, she had taught her how to cook. With dinner being prepared, she would be his dessert, complete with extra toppings such as strawberries, whipped cream, and melted chocolate.

Ebony made sure that Summer would be irresistible. Dressed in an embroidered mesh cut-out sheer lingerie, she was basically wearing dental floss. Ebony also purchased a fifth of Hennessey and told her to man up and don't sip it like a wimp.

As she took a couple of shots straight while watching porn, trying to remember everything Ebony had taught her, she was determined to step out of her comfort zone and win Christopher over. She could see him pulling up on his security camera. She quickly took another larger shot, dropping to her knees as the burning of the alcoholic beverage set her chest on fire. Attempting to gain her composure, she propped herself up on the counter.

Christopher walked into the kitchen with her bent over, stirring her hand in melted chocolate and licking it off her finger. He stood in silence, turned, and proceeded upstairs. Summer was at a loss for words with a bruised ego. She was too tipsy off the Hennessey to make any attempts to make it up the stairs. So, she took a seat at the island in a tipsy stupor and picked up her entire ribeye steak, holding it like a chicken leg, eating it without utensils.

She could hear Christopher coming down the stairs. She jumped up and stood in a sexy pose. He entered the kitchen completely naked, with his body glistening as if he had baby-oiled his entire body. His sizeable manhood was already erect, as if he had started something upstairs without her. He walked into the kitchen and passed her as if he wasn't turned on with her look. Then, he picked up his meal and placed it on the island where she stood. He made deliberate attempts to rub his body against hers as he flexed his muscles. Summer had to make her move before the alcohol wore off, and so did her confidence. She walked behind him and ran her nails lightly down his back.

"What can I do to make you happy?"

She kissed him on his neck, trailing her tongue down his back, kissing around to his chest. Standing on her tiptoes, she gazed into his eyes, and with light pressure, she bit his bottom lip, increasing his sexual arousal.

"Let me make it up, please, baby."

Christopher slightly put his hands around her neck with a sexually tense grip and said, "Say it again."

Summer repeated herself. "Let me make it up to you, please, Daddy."

He picked her up and placed her on the island. Laying her back, he stood between her legs. He squeezed her breasts with one hand while eating his tender steak with the other hand. He slid deep inside of her while still enjoying his meal. He was slow stroking in and out of her while dipping strawberries in the chocolate, then whipped cream, feeding her. He drizzled chocolate over her nipples, taking a handful of her breasts as he sucked every inch of her perky breast clean.

Summer refused to let him dominate the night. She didn't learn all those new tricks to not show him her new skills. She placed her hand on his chest and slowly eased him out of her. She slid down off the island and grabbed the bowl of chocolate. Grabbing him by the hand, she led him to the great room, where she had a chair covered with a towel. She sat him down as she squatted over him and bounced her ass while giving him a lap dance, Christopher's silently giggle at her effort.

It was finally time to sink or swim; she took the bowl of chocolate while holding the shaft of his pulsating cock in her hand, drizzling the chocolate down his lengthy erection. Christopher was impressed by her efforts, so he gave in and let her have her way. She squatted down in front of him and used her entire tongue to lick upwards to the tip of his head. She swirled her tongue around the head before gently bringing it into her mouth.

Ebony's voice was in the back of her head, "Don't stop until all the chocolate is gone." Using her hands, she massages his thick shaft while attempting to master deep throating on her first try. Christopher gathered her hair in his hand, pulling it out of her face as his eyes locked in on her. Looking up at Christopher, she could see he was enjoying it when his head tilted back, and the grip of her hair became tighter. Summer paid close attention to his moans to memorize his highly sensitive areas. His moans became louder as his thrust became faster. Christopher let out a deep growl, stopping her as he stood and used the towel to wash the remaining chocolate from between his thighs. He used his tongue to clean it off her face, throwing her over his shoulders, but they wouldn't make it to the master bedroom.

Instead, they christened the downstairs bedroom. That night, Summer knew she had pleased him in every way, and all was forgiven. They fell asleep in each other's arms with Christopher requesting Summer move in with him and make his house a home.

# CHAPTER 11: DANGER

Summer had a month to sign her lease and start paying rent, or she could take Christopher's offer and move in. Being head over heels in love, she did just that. He paid to have her apartment packed up and everything placed in storage, refusing to allow her to pay for anything. Summer was able to pay off Miss Dangerfield's home in no time. However, Christopher was unaware that she owned the house and had paid for it to be remodeled.

For the first three months, everything was perfect. His family was planning a big birthday bash for him in Malibu, and they'd spend the entire week in California. Summer requested they stay in a hotel because she didn't want to stay in one of Christopher's luxury properties. She was afraid that she might have to stay alone sometimes during this trip, and she didn't want to be alone in a large house where her voice echoed with each word she spoke.

When they arrived in California, Christopher was even more impressed and turned on by Summer's behavior. She shied away from his celebrity friends and chose to stay back at the hotel instead of attending the gathering he hosted. Summer wouldn't meet his family until the night of his party. She thought that was odd, but she remained in her lane. Summer spent most of the time alone in the hotel while Christopher partied from sunup to sundown. He reeked of alcohol daily.

Meanwhile, Ebony introduced Summer to her cousin, who owned a salon in Malibu. Her personality mirrored Ebony's. She was very easygoing, and like Ebony, she scooped Summer up and treated her like family. Sofia was more outgoing than Ebony and didn't take no for an answer. Summer was like the little sister Sofia never had, and she instantly drew a liking to her.

## Birthday Party

Christopher left the hotel at 8:00 a.m. without giving Summer many details, so she enlisted Sofia to do her hair. Her salon was packed. Christopher called multiple times, saying that he had someone coming to the hotel to do her makeup and hair. When Summer informed him, she was with Ebony's cousin getting her hair done, the call disconnected. Summer was unsure if it was a bad connection, so she tried to call him back multiple times. She was getting nervous because she had no outfit yet. And she had no clue of what he had planned because he wasn't answering her calls or texts. On top of that, she was stuck in Sofia's busy salon.

Sofia felt terrible that she picked Summer up and kept her out all day, so she gave her a dress that she had purchased but was too small for her. The dress fit Summer perfectly. She decided to wear the high-low cocktail style off-the-shoulder red dress. The vibrant color of the dress against her skin made her look even more stunning. They spent the rest of the day trying to find shoes that Summer could walk in. With no time to spare, Sofia dropped Summer off at the party. She was so busy playing dress-up; unbeknownst to her, Christopher had arranged for a stylist to style her at the hotel, and he had picked out a black dress for her to wear. All of Christopher's immediate family were dressed in black and white.

Summer called Christopher as soon as she arrived, and he met her in the lobby of the event center. As soon as he laid eyes on her, he looked her up and down in disappointment.

"What the hell are you wearing? So, you just choose to completely disregard what I asked the stylist to dress you in?"

Summer told him that she never made it back to the hotel. His reaction was immediate and intense; he was upset to learn that she had left the hotel and stayed out all day.

"So, this is what you do whenever we are in another state, Huh?"

She didn't want to escalate the situation, so she simply apologized and entered the event on Christopher's arm. She was the only one at the family table in red. His parents were seated at the other end of the long rectangle tables, and Christopher deliberately placed her at the opposite end. Summer remained in the same spot all night, and he never bothered to introduce her to his parents or friends. He spent the evening on the dance floor with a drink in his hand, seemingly oblivious to her presence. However, she didn't make a big deal about it. Hell, her feet were hurting, and she didn't mind not busting her ass on the dance floor. As the night drew to a close, his parents left the building without an introduction by him or his parents.

Christopher spent most of the night conversing with other guests as if she didn't exist.

Meanwhile, Summer wrestled with the thought of going to the restroom because she'd have to walk across the ballroom floor. As she carefully stepped, one of Christopher's guests laughed as he helped her with the door, placing his hand on her lower back. He knew she was soft stepping to prevent from falling. When Summer exited the ladies' room, Christopher was standing outside the door waiting for her. Without saying a word, he walked off and headed to the front of the building.

The doorman asked, "How can I help you, Mr. Diamond? Do you need car service?"

Christopher replied, "No, I'm waiting for the valet to pull around in one of my father's company cars."

"Are you sure you want to drive after drinking so much?" Summer asked.

He didn't respond, standing next to her as if she weren't speaking to him. Knowing he was upset about the dress, she decided to keep quiet for the rest of the night. The valet pulled up in a Mercedes SUV. Christopher hopped in the driver's side and didn't open Summer's door. She got in, and before she could buckle up her seatbelt, he had taken off. He drove around the back of the building and abruptly stopped. Summer paid no attention as she was preoccupied with removing her heels. Suddenly, she felt a painful blow to the left side of her face. He had struck her across her face, causing her head to hit the passenger window.

Summer could hear ringing in her left ear and the taste of blood in her mouth. She felt dazed and shaken up as she looked around to see if another car had hit them. However, that wasn't the case. Her body jerked back into the seat as Christopher pulled off, speeding down the highway and pulling into a convenience store. He jumped out of the SUV and went into the store. Still in shock and afraid, Summer noticed a police car parked on the side of the convenience store. She was terrified of what Christopher would do next. In her state of shock, she decided to request a ride back to the hotel. She opened the door, still dazed from the powerful hit to the face. The officer exited his patrol car and walked to her when he saw her stumbling. She informed him that she had fought with her boyfriend and wasn't trying to press charges; she just needed a ride back to their hotel. She needed to get back before him so she could gather her belongings and fly home.

When Christopher exited the store, the officer informed Summer that due to the swelling to her face, the decision was no longer hers. After placing her in his cruiser barefooted, he walked to the SUV.

Meanwhile, Christopher stepped out, talking on his cell phone while speaking to the officer. He handed the officer his phone to talk with someone on the other line. Summer observed the officer communicating with someone on the phone. The officer returned the phone to Christopher and began walking back to his patrol car. It was at that moment that Summer's eyes were opened, and she truly understood the POWER that the name Diamond carried.

The officer returned to his patrol car, opened Summer's door, and said to her, "I'm sorry for the confusion with you and Mr. Diamond."

Then, he escorted her back to the SUV and told Christopher to have a blessed night. Summer stood outside the passenger door, afraid of the consequences of involving the police officer. Christopher waited until the officer was out of clear view.

"So, bitch, you tried to get me arrested? You know I have been drinking, too. Back the fuck up away from this vehicle."

Summer attempted to grab her purse with her cell in it, but Christopher drew back as if he was about to strike her again. She immediately jumped back, and he drove off quickly, leaving her standing in the store parking lot with no shoes, money, or cell phone.

As she walked into the store barefoot, she used her hand to rake her hair across her face; trembling, cold, and embarrassed, Summer asked the store clerk if she could use the phone. She only knew Ebony's number, so she called her distraught. Ebony was upset and wanted to wire her some money so she could come home. However, Summer had no ID, and she lived with Christopher. Ebony called her cousin, and Sophia quickly came to pick Summer up and dropped her off at the hotel at Summer's request two hours after being abandoned by Christopher. She begged Summer to just come home with her. However, her entire life existed with Christopher now, and she felt she had no choice but to return to the hotel.

Christopher left her tapping at the door for fifteen minutes before he opened it. Shaking with fear and feeling scared of the unknown, she walked into the hotel room and took a seat in the chair. Christopher laid across the bed and turned off the lights, making the room pitch black. Summer's feet were dirty and gritty; she had dry blood around her mouth with a pounding headache. She needed to shower but feared him cornering her in the bathroom. She debated if she should shower. She thought to herself that he was bipolar and clearly had a mental issue. He was lying in the bed as if he didn't just punch her like he was fighting another man.

Summer quietly made her way to the bathroom and closed the door behind her. Her eyes fixed on the door as she sat in the tub with the shower running, sobbing in disbelief. After her shower, she slowly eased open the bathroom door, slowly soft stepping, and tried to feel her way around in the dark to avoid waking Christopher up when he called out to her.

"Summer," Christopher called out.

"Yes, Christopher."

"Come lay down," he demanded.

She tried to tell him that she was trying to find her night clothes when he sat up in bed and yelled, "I said come lay down now!!"

Summer crawled into bed with a towel wrapped around her. He pulled her to him, forcing her into a spooning position as he placed his hand around her neck. Summer immediately began to cry harder.

"I'm sorry. Please, Christopher," she said as his grip around her throat tightened.

As he squeezed her around her throat, he said, "Next time you try to pull that shit again, I will crush your damn windpipe."

Summer's body trembled in fear; she was afraid to speak. Who was he? This is not the man she fell in love with.

"Do you hear me?" he asked as he choked her harder.

"Yes, Christopher. I'm sorry," she cried out.

"Yes, who?" he asked.

"Yes, sir," she said, holding his hand, trying to loosen his grip.

I said, "Yes, who?"

"Yes, Daddy," Summer replied as he loosened his grip.

"That's better, and by the way, if I wanted to introduce my family to a whore in a tight dress, I could have easily brought someone from my past."

Christopher was upset because he had bragged to his dad about this wholesome young lady, he had met who changed his life. He had taken the time to present her a certain way, but when Summer arrived, revealing too much skin, depleting the image he had set in his mind.

That night, Summer slept with Christopher's hand around her throat.

The following morning, exhausted from the fight, Christopher had left the room while Summer was sleeping. When she opened her eyes and touched her neck, she could feel the left side of her face throbbing in pain. She looked around the room and didn't see Christopher. She spotted a Trumpet/Mermaid scoop neck asymmetrical stretch crepe evening dress with beading sequins. The dress was stunning. Christopher even had the perfect low-heeled designer shoes that she could walk in. He had put a lot of effort into presenting her well to his parents.

In some way, Summer understood why Christopher was upset. However, she could never understand or condone his actions after the party. She stood in the mirror, crying and looking at her swollen, bruised face, when Christopher walked in and found her in the bathroom. He tried to converse as if last night didn't happen. But Summer was waiting for an apology. He had sobered up, and surely, when he saw what he had done to her face, he'd be begging for her forgiveness. Instead, it was quite the opposite. He grabbed her from behind while squeezing her breast and looking at her in the mirror.

He said, "I hope you have makeup to cover that bruise."

Then, he kissed her on the forehead before he walked out of the bathroom. Summer was speechless as she attempted to cover the bruise. However, her shade of makeup was too light and didn't conceal it well. They were leaving for the airport in an hour, so she combed her hair toward her face and wore a baseball cap and shades that she purchased from the hotel gift shop. She started to second-guess her relationship, feeling like she made a mistake moving in. She had given up everything to move in with Christopher.

## CHAPTER 12: *Returning to the Unknown*

Summer felt humiliated as she returned home. She didn't meet Christopher's parents, she had a busted face, and she was possibly living with an abuser. Just the thought of having to face Ebony at work the next day was gut-wrenching.

Summer couldn't continue to live like this. She needed to understand why Christopher thought it was acceptable to hit her. Adding insult to injury, he left her stranded in unfamiliar surroundings out of state without a care. After settling in and unpacking her bags, she joined him in the family room, where he was watching TV. She sat opposite of him on a different sofa.

"Can we talk?" she asked.

He paused the movie, sat back in the chair, and crossed his arms. "What's up?"

Summer played with her nails, looking down at the floor. She finally made eye contact with him. He sat looking at her with a blank expression.

"Christopher are you really okay with what you did to me?" she asked, her voice trembling.

He stood, pulled the ottoman forward, and placed it to sit facing her. Not trusting his reactions anymore, she was immediately timid, and her body tensed slightly.

"Ask your question again," he said, staring with a lack of emotions.

Summer began to stutter before she burst into tears, asking, "How could you treat me like that?"

"Okay," he said. "Can you tell me everything you did to me before you pushed me over the edge?"

Summer looked confused as he made her recall everything she had done to hurt him. She left the hotel without communicating, disregarded any effort or time he spent to make her feel beautiful, and on top of coming to his party in front of his parents dressed in the wrong colors, she was dressed like a whore, showing too much skin and allowing another man's hands all over her. Christopher had watched as one of his guests caressed her back, and he instantly saw red. In two minutes, he had made her pain about him, turning himself into the victim.

Summer was speechless when he refused to take any responsibility or show any remorse. She leans back on the sofa with tears streaming down her face.

"Are we done?" he asked in a sarcastic tone.

"Yes, Christopher. I am done."

He returned to the chair and resumed the movie while watching Summer out of the corner of his eyes as she looked disgusted with him. He turned off the TV and grabbed her by the hand.

"Come to the bedroom. I'm going to allow you to smother me."

Summer quickly snatched her hand back, although it was tempting to put a pillow over his face and smother the hell out of him for the way her face looked. Still, she wasn't amused by his games.

"No, I'm serious. Come on," Christopher insisted.

He forcefully pulled her by her hand and led her to the bedroom.

"I want you to smother me."

As he attempted to pull her dress off, Summer quickly realized that he just wanted sex. So, she turned and attempted to go back downstairs. He wrestled her to the bed and ripped her panties off, roaring as she tried to fight him off. She pushes and tugs at his shirt, trying to fight him off.

"No, you're mad at me," he said as he laughed, knowing she couldn't match his strength.

"Get even. Sit on my face and smother me," Christopher repeated.

Then, he forcefully flipped her over on top of him and made her squat over him, pinning his arms around her thighs as he stuffed his face between her thighs.

"Sit on my face until I can't breathe."

After much resistance, Summer gave in to Christopher's amazing oral sex as he managed to manipulate his tongue between her folds. Guiding her hips as she rode his face, he grabbed her by her waist and slid her down, positioning her on his throbbing erection.

Summer was caught up in lust as he stroked deeper, asking if she forgave him. He stroked deeper and deeper, faster and faster, until her legs were shaking, and she was screaming, "I forgive you, I forgive you," as she climaxed. Summer lay next to Christopher after he had used sex as an apology. She was disappointed and mad with herself; his sex was irresistible, and she knew that she had just cosigned his reckless behavior.

Later that night, she called Ebony and asked if she could show up early to work and bring her makeup bag to help cover her bruise. Ebony agreed and showed up as promised. However, even with great effort, she was unable to cover the bruise completely. Ebony didn't ask for any details; she only wanted to know if Summer was safe to remain in his home. Summer fed her lies about Christopher's remorse. She claimed that the alcohol that he had consumed all week played a big part in his actions. Ebony, feeling empathetic and partially guilty, didn't push the issue.

Summer skipped the Monday morning meeting and remained in her office the entire day. She waited until her morning shift had left the building before leaving. She tried taking the stairs to avoid everyone else but ran into Stevin. She couldn't hide her bruises from him. He touched her face to comfort her.

"Is there anything I can do to assist you?" Stevin asked.

"No, I'm okay. I just have two left feet," Summer said as she tried to ease past him down the stairs.

Stevin grabbed her by the hand and stopped her.

"I will forever kick myself for not truly telling you my true feelings."

Then, he kissed the back of her hand and exited the stairway. Not wanting to rock the boat, she kept their run-in to herself.

When she returned home, Christopher had dinner prepared for her. He even drew her a bath and insisted on bathing her as he massaged her body while she relaxed. He pampered her for the next month and made sure that his love for her wasn't in question. There was no mention of meeting his parents again, but she was happy just being with him, ignoring all the warning signs.

*Dream Crusher: Two Years In*

While cuddling on the sofa watching a movie, Summer jokingly asked Christopher if he would still find her attractive when she is big and pregnant like the actress in the movie. His response crushed Summer's world.

"We don't have to worry about that because we won't be having kids."

Summer sat straight up to look at him, thinking he was joking. However, he wasn't.

"I don't want kids," he added.

He'd just delivered a blow that she couldn't accept.

"Christopher, that's not fair to me. I want kids."

"The answer is no," he retorted. "You can change the subject. My answer will not change."

"No, I won't change the subject. This is not fair to me. You don't wait and divulge something like this to me two years into our relationship. I want kids. This changes everything; I mean, this is a game-changer.

He leaped off the sofa, loomed over Summer, and his voice rose in intensity. "What's a game-changer?" He grabbed her by her shirt and asked in an aggressive tone, "I said repeat yourself. Believe one damn thing! Your ass is not going anywhere, and not one kid will be pushed out of you. What the hell do you want kids for? Look at you! No family! You have no idea who your worthless parents are, and you want to bring a child into this world with no family history."

Summer was speechless that he would speak to her in this manner. She attempted to exit the room, but Christopher grabbed a handful of her hair and slung her to the floor.

"Do we have an issue?" he asked as he pinned her to the floor and placed his body weight on her.

Afraid of being hit, she struggled with him and tried to cover her face while crying out, "Christopher, please. I just want to go to bed, please."

He released her, and she ran upstairs, calling him an asshole. Instantly, she knew that she had let her anger put her in a position that she'd regret. When she saw Christopher jump off the sofa to run after her, she knew at that moment that she had fucked up. So, she quickly ran into the bedroom and hid in the large walk-in closet in the corner behind his clothes. She could hear him going from room to room, searching for her. As silence filled the house, she balled up in the corner of the closet, shaking, holding her mouth, and praying that he couldn't hear her panting in fear as she tried to avoid making any noise. She was startled as he grabbed her by the ankle and dragged her out of the closet.

She kicked and screamed, "I'm sorry! I'm sorry! I didn't mean it, Christopher."

However, her apology and tears didn't hold back his raw emotions as she felt blows to the back of her head. Summer turned on her side with one arm in the air, trying to block the punches and avoid being hit in her face. It felt as if he was hitting her with a blunt object. The blows were so painful. He yanked her up and threw her on the bed as he continued to hit her with his closed fist. She prayed that the beating would stop as she attempted to pin her body against his to decrease the force of his punches. Christopher grabbed her by the neck and forbade her to leave the bedroom as he screamed in her face. Summer balled up in bed in shock that he just beat her like he had no love in his heart for her. Her body was in extreme pain; she was afraid to move and, even more, worried that he might return and start pouncing on her again. She just lay quietly in her own blood and drool.

It was hours later before Christopher returned to the bedroom. He climbed into bed next to her as if he didn't just beat her like a nappy-headed stepchild. Summer's body is shocked by pain. Her head was pounding as she cried and sniffled while lying in fear of the unknown.

He rudely said, "I can't sleep if you can't stop making all that damn noise. Go sleep in one of the guest rooms."

Her body was stiff and too painful to move. It ached with every clench of her muscles as she dragged herself to another bedroom. Summer entered the bathroom, trying to clean herself up while avoiding looking at her appearance in the mirror. She couldn't bring herself to look at her bruised, battered body. After cleaning herself up, she quietly crawled into bed, still fearing Christopher's rage. She lay daydreaming of the warmth and comfort of Miss Dangerfield's hugs. Then, she cried herself to sleep, feeling hopeless in the relationship.

The next morning, Summer called in sick to work because she woke up with bruises all over her body and large knots in the back of her head. She wanted to avoid Christopher at all costs, so she stayed in bed in the guest room as long as possible. She could hear doors opening and closing, assuming he was going around the house searching for her. Suddenly, she heard the door open to the room she was in. He entered the bedroom and sat next to her on the bed.

"Do you want to talk?" he asked.

When she refused to answer, he knelt before her to be at eye level and gently held her hand, stroking her face with tears in his eyes. Emotionally drained, Summer wailed while avoiding looking at him. Christopher crawled into bed, holding her and making sniffling noises behind her head as if he were crying. Eventually, Summer fell asleep. It wasn't that she found comfort in his arms, but the fact that she didn't have to worry about being attacked. Summer came to the realization that Christopher was not the perfect Prince Charming he portrayed himself to be in the beginning. The idea that she might never have the opportunity to start a family and experience every joyful moment of raising a child and overcompensating in all areas her childhood lacked had soured on her. She could never have imagined feeling so disconnected and powerless in her relationship with Christopher.

As months passed, the growing disconnection became more and more apparent. Summer's behavior seemed robotic, and she felt like a stranger in her own body. She did anything to keep the peace. Her needs and wants were whatever Christopher desired.

Christopher, in turn, noticed the significant disconnect as there was no authentic affection from Summer. Intimacy felt forced, lacking passion, and there was no sexual thrill as Summer laid on her back and daydreamed that she was anywhere but underneath him. Christopher truly loved Summer; seeing her experience the world from a different perspective was a thrill for him. He found solace in introducing her to a world that she could have never known without him. It was a knife to his heart, and he felt as if Summer was slowly slipping away, no longer seeing him as her protector or that knight in shining armor who swept her off her feet. Determined to win her back, he was ready to acknowledge his mistakes and prove that his love was unwavering.

As Summer sat at her desk, she daydreamed about Miss Dangerfield's memorial tree. She imagined herself lying in the yard under the tree, staring at the sky, and having an intimate moment with Mimi. She spent hours contemplating how she'd spend her upcoming vacation. With two weeks off, the thought of spending every moment in Christopher's home with him made her ill. She needed to devise a plan to return to her hometown, knowing Christopher could never know that she not only saved Miss Dangerfield's home, but she also owned it. Determined to spend a week at home during her vacation, she just needed the perfect lie that he wouldn't question.

While she was lost in her thoughts, Ebony knocked on her office door, inviting her to lunch.

Summer replied, "Only if we can eat alone."

"Anything for you, Bae," Ebony replied, using the endearing term they had adopted for each other over the years.

Summer made sure to choose a quiet restaurant and asked to be seated away from other customers. As she sat with her head down, Ebony touched her hand.

"Summer, I'm here. Whatever you need, I'm here for you."

Looking up with tears in her eyes, she asked, "Did you know, Ebony? Did you know?"

Ebony sat quietly with a puzzled look on her face. She was caught off guard by Summer's question.

However, she dropped her head and said, "Yes, but I promise I didn't know it could get this bad. Please don't let this interfere with our friendship," she pleaded.

Finally, she broke her silence and told Summer why she was so against her dating Christopher. She had warned her from the start not to get involved with him. Ebony had only seen a small preview of his rage. He had previously dated her neighbor, who was well-established and had family support. She told Summer of encounters where Christopher tried to isolate his ex, but her family stepped in. When he couldn't control her or make her detach from her parents, he used his father's power and money to destroy her credit and reputation until she picked up and moved to another state.

"Summer, I believed that he had changed. I honestly thought you had changed him. He never stopped seeing other women when he was dating Trish. He just needed to control her. The love and compassion he showed towards you made me feel at ease. But now, I feel I betrayed you.

"Summer, there's more. Christopher's father bankrolls my husband's companies. If his father walked, all of Thomas's contracts would vanish. Trish was one of my closest friends, and I witnessed firsthand who Mr. Christopher Diamond really was after he ruined my friend's life.

"Christopher was concerned about his reputation, and he threatened my husband by nicely reminding him that with just one phone call, all of Thomas's clients would walk. In so many words, he said that if I didn't keep quiet, he would bankrupt Thomas's entire company.

"Over the past year, my husband's biggest clients have been coming into town to meet with Christopher for a drink and cigars. Thomas had already warned me to keep my mouth shut and my opinions to myself.

"Summer, the Diamond name is powerful, and Christopher has used every ounce to his advantage."

Ebony spent the rest of the lunch begging and pleading for Summer's silence. Summer wasn't mad at Ebony. She felt that it was her fault alone for not listening to any of Ebony's warnings before she got entangled with Christopher Diamond.

## CHAPTER 13: A LITTLE BIT OF SUNSHINE

Summer started having nightmares about Christopher. She was pretty sure that the nightmares were related to the information she received from Ebony, as it consumed her every thought. She began to see Christopher as the enemy. She thought that if she had not been so blind to all his charms and lies, she probably would have paid more attention to Mimi's illness, and her life could have been different. She reflected on the final months of Miss Dangerfield's life and the obvious signs that she was ill.

Summer stood in the kitchen preparing Christopher's dinner, wondering how much rat poison she could sprinkle on his food. She wanted to use just enough to make him severely ill and be undetectable so that it wouldn't land her in prison.

As she contemplated his fate, Christopher walked in and kissed her on the back of her neck. She cringed as his hands touched her. He dropped his head and walked upstairs. At that moment, he knew he had lost her. He laid back on the bed, thinking of his next move. The fear of losing her was too much to bear. He wanted her next to him by any means necessary, but most of all, he wanted that look in her eyes back. He wanted to see that look as if he were everything she wanted and needed.

He decided to walk back downstairs to talk to Summer.

"Turn the fire off on the stove," he requested, and then he took her by the hand and sat her at the table. "Summer, I need you to open your heart up to me, and please hear me out. Can you please just do that for me?"

Summer didn't say anything, so he continued.

"Do you still love me?"

She wanted to jump up from the table, slap him, and scream, "Hell no, fool!" But her heart was a battleground of conflicting emotions. Instead, she dropped her head with a slight shoulder shrug as if she didn't know.

Christopher shifted in his seat and moved his body closer to the table. Summer's heart skipped a beat, fearing the punches that were about to occur. He placed his elbows on the table and covered his face as he began to rub up and down his nose, using both index fingers to wipe the tears out of the corner of his eyes.

"Summer, I didn't know life could be this happy until you walked into my life. I would be a fool if I didn't believe I owe you a million apologies. I haven't been transparent with you, and I haven't loved you as you should be loved. If you want to walk away now and leave this relationship without hearing me out, I promise I won't stop you." His regret hung heavy in the air.

"Really?" she thought to herself. She imagined herself leaping from the table, dashing upstairs, gathering a handful of clothes, and fleeing. But the fear of it being a ploy, coupled with Ebony's cautionary tale, left her paralyzed. ·

"You grew up in this world not knowing who your parents are. You felt lost and abandoned. I was born with a silver spoon in my mouth, knowing both of my parents. Yet I felt lost and abandoned my entire life."

He went on to tell her about his childhood and being raised by a wealthy alcoholic mother who was never present. He had a rich and powerful father who used money and gifts for love and affection. As a kid, when he yearned for love and attention from his parents, his father would call him weak.

Later in life, he learned from his oldest brother during an argument that his father was the reason he lost his virginity at the age of fifteen. He had paid Chris's 25-year-old live-in nanny to sleep with him because his father felt he was too soft and needed to become a man.

"They're not fit to be parents; they don't deserve grandkids," he repeated over and over again.

He told Summer he despised his father and wanted to be nothing like him.

"Do you know what it feels like to have your mom living in the same house with you as a kid and not be allowed to see her? Never receiving a hug from her. Are these the people you want me to bless with a grandchild? My older siblings are so brainwashed. My father runs every aspect of their lives. I'm the black sheep of the family because I moved away and dug my father's claws out of my back. I have never done anything right in his eyes. My brother's wives are purchased Stepford wives who earn bankrolls to play their parts while their husbands pretend to have a powerful role in the company when they're really only my father's puppets.

"Summer, you were real. You are real! I found true love, someone so perfect and pure. I knew God sent you to me that night in the club. It's like you were the only soul present. I couldn't keep my eyes off of you. I honestly knew I was falling for you the moment you looked me in my eyes. I'd give anything for you to look at me like that again. I know your vacation starts on Monday. I'm begging you to take a trip with me overseas for a week."

Summer quickly rebutted, "Christopher, I really wanted to fly home alone and spread Mimi's ashes next week. Besides, I never want to go back to the Bahamas. It's too painful to think about revisiting the place where I was when I lost her."

"Please Summer, I want to take you to Bora Bora. I already have everything booked. Just give me this one thing, and if you want to fly back home or walk away from this relationship when we return, I won't stop you. Please just give me this one thing before you give up completely on me. Please, Summer."

Summer remained silent, looking down at the floor, her face devoid of any emotion. Christopher was crushed by her apparent lack of emotions. In a sudden burst of frustration, he jumped up from his seat, slamming his hands on the table.

"Fuck it, Summer!" he shouted. "I get it. It's over; you're not in love with me. I'll just leave and stay in a hotel until you find a place if that's what makes you comfortable," he declared as he stormed off.

Summer, still emotionless, stood and walked into the kitchen to finish her dinner. In disbelief, and heartbroken by her reaction, Christopher walked up behind her grabbing her and pleaded for her attention. He begged her to look him in the eyes and tell him that she doesn't love him. She dropped her head with her forehead resting on his chest. He picked her up and placed her on the island, forcing eye contact.

"Look me in my eyes and tell me it's over," he implored, his voice trembling with desperation.
Summer's heart was suddenly flooded with a mix of emotions. For the first time in months, she found herself feeling something for him, unable to ignore Christopher's heartache and the pain in his eyes.

"Baby, I'm begging you, please tell me the truth. Do you not love me?" he asked again.

Looking up in his sexy grayish-brown eyes was like looking through a window of pain filled with raindrops of tears. Her brick wall collapsed, and the emotions and love she had spent months burying started flooding her heart and thoughts as she emotionally broke down. Christopher embraced her with a hug and a kiss while pleading for her forgiveness and love. He could feel her body relax; she was no longer tense to his touch. He felt her guard dropping as she allowed herself to be cradled in his arms. Christopher couldn't remember the last time she had felt so relaxed in his embrace. He just held her and savored the moment.

Summer lifted her head and agreed to go. Then, she told him that she needed a moment alone.

"I think I need to take a drive and clear my head."

Christopher played it safe and didn't take any chance of screwing the moment up. He simply kissed her on the forehead and released her.

"Okay. I'm headed to bed."

Summer got into her car and drove far enough down the hill to get out of the view of Christopher's security cameras. She called Ebony to seek advice, detailing Christopher's raw emotions.

Summer explained that she somewhat understood his reason for not wanting kids and sought Ebony's advice on what she should do. Ebony suggested that Summer should only take the trip if she felt safe and use the time to clear her mind and figure out what she really wanted. When Summer returned home, she found Christopher lying in bed. She really didn't want to go on the trip, making the decision to request that they work out whatever they needed to at home. She turned on the lamp to tell him her decision; Christopher looked up, appearing defeated and lost, which broke her heart. At that moment, all she wanted to do was give him peace. She turned off the lamp, got into bed on his side, and rested her head on his arm. He hugged her tightly while smelling her hair and kissing her shoulder as if he'd just received his world back. Summer fell asleep in Christopher's arms and actually slept peacefully for the first time in months.

*Love is in the Air*

When they arrived in Bora Bora, Summer couldn't deny that it was breathtaking. Christopher was so humble; everything was about keeping Summer happy. Exhausted from the long travel, Summer just wanted to eat, shower, and sleep. It was 9:42 p.m. back in the States but 4:42 p.m. in Bora Bora. Christopher had no objection. Trying to adjust to the time difference, Summer asked Christopher to wake her in two hours. He allowed her to sleep as requested, and then he awakened her with soft kisses to her lips.

After freshening up, she was led through the private bungalow to the spa to receive a massage. The beauty of the ocean, visible through the glass-bottom peekaboo floors, was awe-inspiring as she lay on the massage table.

After much-needed pampering, Summer spent the rest of the evening in Christopher's arms overlooking the tropical beachfront. No words were spoken, as it was clear that they both just needed to take in the moment while it lasted. The night came to a close, so Summer headed to take a shower to prepare for bed. The shower was amazing. It was located in an open area in the middle of the bathroom with a large rainfall and mist thermostatic shower head. She was enjoying all the different water settings as Christopher walked up, grabbed her from behind, and started to wash her body. He gently washed her body while deeply massaging her muscles with every touch. Not wanting to push too fast, he kissed her forehead and then attempted to walk off.

However, Summer's body was craving for his touch and wanted him to take her and do what he pleased with her body. Her beautiful surroundings, the serene atmosphere, and the fact it had been months since she allowed herself to enjoy his touch.

She grabbed him by the hand, indicating that she wanted him to stay. He passionately grabbed a handful of her wet hair and kissed her to complete arousal of all her sexual senses. Christopher lifted her off her feet as she wrapped her legs around his waist. He carried her to the bed, but they never unlocked their lips. They made love throughout the night; Christopher felt that sexual vulnerability from Summer that always drove his sex drive to the next level. He explored every inch of her body until she passed out from sexual pleasure. Christopher watched her sleep, lying next to her, gently rubbing and kissing her body.

Hours later, Christopher was awakened by Summer lying beside him, rubbing his cheek, her face streaked with tears. He opened his eyes wider to focus on her, but he was afraid to question her about her feelings and why she was crying. Summer touched his cheek and said, "Please promise me you won't disappear."

He looked confused as she repeated herself.

"This Christopher. You're the man I fell in love with. Please promise me this man lying next to me won't change. I never want to see the other side of you. If so, I will walk away and never look back."

Taking her hand and kissing it, he remained silent, wiping the tears from her eyes. He pulled her on top of him, feeling her warmth and her fear. She laid her head on his chest, listening to every beat of his heart. Without him speaking a word, she felt his sincerity. She eventually fell asleep lying on top of him, feeling safe in his embrace.

When morning came, she was confused when she woke up alone. She wondered how he managed to move her off him without waking her. Christopher had left a note with a beautiful flowing white dress and a Tiare Tahiti flower that she was instructed to pin in her hair. She got dressed and waited for his return. He slipped in, snuck up behind her, and covered her eyes.

She giggled and asked, "What are you doing?"

"Do you trust me?" he asked.

Summer nodded yes as Christopher placed a blindfold over her eyes. He turned her to face him, gently kissed her, and told her how beautiful and pure she looked. Feeling his soft lips and enjoying his seductive fragrance, she eagerly anticipated being handcuffed to the bed. She'd hoped he'd rip the dress off her and have his way. Instead, they began to walk, and she could feel the sand between her toes. She was puzzled about the secrecy as he stopped to remove the blindfold but asked her to keep her eyes closed and not open them until he told her to. She could feel him step away as the sweet sound of a violin started to play.

"Open your eyes, Summer," he said.

Summer opened her eyes to a beautiful sunset overlooking the ocean with a musician on the beach playing the violin. Beach lanterns lit up the beach, and Tiare Tahiti flowers were spread along the pathway.

She turned to locate Christopher, who was standing behind her. He was dressed in all white and down on one knee, holding a three-karat round infinity engagement ring surrounded in 14k white gold. Speechless, she dropped to her knees and wept with joy as he held her hand and slid the ring on her ring finger.

Summer could have never imagined being proposed to in this manner. It was beyond anything she could have dreamed of, yet, within that same breath, it was great sadness. She wasn't ready to give up on her dream of having kids. But in that moment, Summer's heart was filled with overwhelming joy, which she had never experienced before, even as she grappled with the sadness of her unfulfilled dream of having kids.

Christopher thought of everything; his meticulous planning was evident in every detail. He had even arranged for a photographer to capture the moment. With a romantic dinner set up on the beach, they sat under the moonlight as the beach lanterns cast a mesmerizing reflection on the ocean water.

Summer couldn't tell which scenery shined the most beautifully as she kept holding her hand up, waving it back and forth, admiring her ring. She looked up at Christopher, who was watching her with a big heartwarming smile.

"Baby, can I please use my phone to call Ebony and tell her the news."

Christopher was glad she was happy, so he didn't mind if she shouted it to the world. He scooped her up and carried her into the cold ocean waters as she screamed in laughter.

Finally, they returned to the bungalow and undressed each other before they showered. They stood under the warm shower water together as he made love to her naked body, which was clothed only in her beautiful diamond engagement ring.

They retreated to the bed, and Christopher quickly fell asleep. Sometime later, he woke up and found himself alone. He jumped out of bed, searched for Summer, and discovered her alone on the beach. He took her by the hand and led her back inside. He sensed that something was wrong when she wouldn't look up. He guided her to sit on the bed and gently lifted her head to make eye contact. It was evident that she had been crying.

"Tell me what's wrong, baby," he said.

Summer shook her head no. She was afraid to be honest and ruin this perfect day.

"Do you not want to marry me?" he asked as he dropped his head.

"No..., I want to marry you," she paused. "But, why can't we have a child and start our own tradition? You are not your father. I'm not your mother. Why do they control how we'd be as parents? She wept.

Christopher placed his hand over his face and then laid backwards on the bed as the room went silent. Summer laid her head on his chest.

"Baby, just think about it. That's all I ask. Please just let our love for each other be your determining factor."

As he gently pushed her off of him, Christopher sat up and said, "I'm not saying yes, but I'm not saying no. If I decide to go through with it, it has to be planned through and through and not forced on me. I don't want to discuss this anymore until after the wedding when we have traveled and enjoyed our life together as husband and wife." His struggle with the decision was evident in his voice and the way he avoided her gaze.

Summer leaped onto his lap, kissing him. In her mind, that was Christopher saying yes to them having a child in the future. As she lay beside him in his arms, the only missing component was Mimi. But Summer knew she was her guardian angel. She consciously decided to fully embrace her new engagement and give Christopher her undivided attention, so she would wait until she returned home to talk to Ebony. Summer spent the rest of her time in Bora Bora, ensuring Christopher was happy and satisfied. She returned home with lockjaw and a temporary stank walk, but all that mattered was that Christopher had a permanent smile.

# CHAPTER 14: A New Beginning

Summer returned to work with engagement photos and her new diamond ring. The sparkle of the diamond reflected her happiness as she bragged to Ebony about how Christopher was a changed man and how perfect he was. Her eyes sparkled with love, a pleasant sight to Ebony.

Ebony had not slept in months. She was worried about Summer's emotional state, feeling consumed by guilt. Although Christopher was still the enemy, she knew she had to allow Summer to make her own choices.

They spent the week browsing through bridal magazines and creating a vision board for her wedding. Ebony even began spending time at Christopher's home. He didn't mind one bit, as long as Ebony was in favor of the wedding and her time in his home was spent planning the wedding; he was okay with her being there. The only problem was that Summer didn't have a date for the wedding. Christopher kept avoiding the conversation, saying he needed to check his family schedules and that he would possibly have his father clear the schedule for next year around the summertime.

Summer questioned Christopher as to why his family needed to attend, suggesting she'd be okay with a destination wedding. This angered Christopher that she would suggest that. He countered her question with why she had been spending so much time with

Ebony planning for a church wedding if she truly wanted to elope on a private beach and get married without friends or family. Not wanting to cause any conflict, Summer stopped asking for a date. Life was improving for her, and she just wanted to savor the moment.

Summer was not only engaged, but Stevin had also recommended her for a new position as a nurse recruiter. Excited about the opportunity, she said yes to Stevin before discussing it with Christopher. Astonishingly, he was supportive - even with the fact that she'd have to travel occasionally for the job. Christopher was only so agreeable because it gave her something new to focus on. Besides, he'd rather drag the engagement out a little longer. Summer sensed that he wasn't completely honest with her about his feelings regarding a short engagement. She just dropped the subject and focused on her new position.

Two weeks into training, Summer came home from work and noticed that Christopher had removed her wedding planning book and her vision board from the office and put everything in the storage area outside in the garage. She was confused and hurt and demanded answers. She returned to the office and asked Christopher why he'd put the wedding plans away.

"Are you having second thoughts? Or are you too embarrassed of me?" she cried.

"What the fuck are you talking about, Summer?" he replied as he walked off and headed to the master bedroom.

Fueled by her anger, she continued to press for answers. She followed him into the walk-in closet as he sat down and put on a pair of shoes. Summer was hurt and led by frustration with his lack of support in planning their wedding.

She stared at him momentarily and then blurted out, "Are you embarrassed of me because I don't have any family that will be at the wedding?"

"You better get the hell out of here," Christopher shouted, jumping up from the closet chair and aggressively approaching her.

Summer's facial expression went from anger to fear as she stumbled backward, afraid of what Christopher might do.

"What the hell are you saying?" he yelled.

"If you're so damn bright, tell me something. Did I propose to you before or after I learned that you had no family?"

Summer dropped her head.

"Exactly," he said. "You don't have to leave. I'm getting the hell out of here."

He sped down the driveway, leaving home at 6:00 p.m. Despite several calls and texts from Summer, he didn't respond. He finally returned home at 2 a.m. When he entered their bedroom, Summer was sitting up in bed with her knees pulled up to her chest and her arms wrapped around her knees. She had a few hours before work, and her eyes were puffy from crying. She had no interest in fighting with Christopher. She was happy that he was home safe, and she was also afraid to question his whereabouts. She turned over and faced the wall with her back towards him. He could feel her body jerking with every sniff as she tried to hide her emotions.

"I wasn't with a woman, Summer. I wasn't with anyone," he said. "I wouldn't cheat on you. I don't care how mad I get; I wouldn't cheat on you. And I don't care what date you set for the wedding."

Summer didn't reply. She was too heartbroken. The thought of Christopher slipping back into his old ways made her ill. She finally fell asleep one hour before it was time to awaken and prepare for work.

*Wishing She Were Anywhere but Work*

While sitting at her desk, Summer heard a tap at the door. It was Stevin. She had purposely avoided contact with everyone today because she looked like hell. When Stevin saw her red, puffy eyes, he asked her if taking the new position was a bad idea. She reassured him that her job would not be affected and that she only canceled today's training because she was ill and had been up all night without sleep. She had no desire to defend her disheveled appearance or her lack of enthusiasm for work. So, she put on her sunglasses, packed up her case files, and requested to leave early. She walked out of her office with Stevin. They entered the elevator together and left the unit. Summer was so caught up in her drama with Christopher that she never noticed Amber watching her and Stevin talking and leaving together.

She took her case files home and planned to spend the next two days working from home. She was still upset about Christopher's poor decision last night. So, she just dropped her files on the office desk and headed to the shower, then to bed at three in the evening. Christopher was upset when he noticed she intentionally avoided speaking to him and never returned downstairs to fix dinner for him. After waiting hours for her to return downstairs, he walked upstairs at 7:00 p.m. and attempted to wake her. He asked her when she was coming down to fix dinner. She remained silent, never opening her eyes as she slept. He finally fixed himself a ham sandwich for dinner, livid that she'd ignored him.

After his light dinner, Christopher walked into the bedroom, flipping lights on and knocking around items. He tried to do anything that would disturb Summer's sleep. Choosing to continue to ignore him, she pulled the covers over her head and fell back to sleep. He climbed into bed next to her and fell asleep within the hour. Summer was even more upset with him and aggravated by his antics with the lights and noise earlier. So, she used the remote control to drop the A.C. to 50 degrees. Then, she turned up the ceiling fan and eased the blanket off of him. He shivered throughout the night and snuggled deeper underneath the blanket. When he doze off again, she would ease the blanket off him again. When he began to sneeze, she turned all the settings back to the typical setting and eased the remote control back on the nightstand. She was startled by Christopher suddenly grabbing her. He never opened his eyes as he pulled her close and used her body heat to warm up. Summer fell back to sleep with a big smile on her face.

The next morning, Christopher awakened, confused about why Summer was downstairs working in the office instead of at work. He entered the kitchen and noticed she hadn't attempted to make breakfast for him. He then returned to the office and stood in the doorway. After a few seconds, Summer looked up and made eye contact with him.

"I'm going upstairs to get dressed. I'm expecting breakfast when I return back downstairs," he said in a demanding tone.

Then, he walked off, sniffing and sneezing. Summer stuck her tongue out, silently laughing at her antics with the thermostat during the night. When Christopher returned to the kitchen, she was finishing up his Eggs Benedict. She turned to walk out of the kitchen without verbally addressing him. Christopher grabbed her by the arm and made her face him as he wrapped his arms around her.

"You can be mad. I will give you that, but please tell me you believe me when I tell you I wouldn't cheat on you."

"Christopher, I understand that every day won't be lollipops and flowers, but to shit on my parade - my happiness that is occurring because of your actions... Without any reason, your entire mood and attitude change suddenly. Then, when I have questions, your response is to storm out and cut off all communication. Yeah, I'm lost," she said.

"I told you the other night, go ahead and pick the date. I went to the club and completed some paperwork to clear my head. You want to plan a wedding, start a new job, etc. Move at your own pace, Summer. If you think you can do it all, I will support it."

Summer walked off and returned to the office feeling like Christopher was still hiding his true feelings. Nevertheless, she followed up with Ebony. He could hear her asking for Ebony's opinion on a summer wedding. They immediately jumped back into wedding mode, excited about finally having a precise month. For the next two weeks, every conversation she started with Christopher was related to the wedding: color, flowers, location, etc. He started throwing himself into new projects to avoid the conversation, forcing her to make decisions on her own.

# CHAPTER 15: IS IT CHRISTOPHER OR CHRIS?

Summer was unfazed by Christopher's occasional ambivalence about their wedding. One week, he was willing to give his opinion, and the next week, he was wishy-washy. She decided to take charge of all the wedding plans on her own and only to involve him when she needed him to swipe his black card.

One day, while out shopping with Ebony, she returned home and overheard Christopher on the phone arguing with one of his siblings. It turned out his father had learned about his engagement through one of Thomas's clients and was upset that he hadn't approved of Christopher and Summer's wedding. He informed Christopher that because his father had no say in the wedding, he had forbidden anyone to talk to him until he agreed to meet with his father.

Summer hesitated to ask any questions. She had learned to stay clear of conversations that involved Christopher and his father. Moments later, he stormed out the door and left without saying anything to her. Summer texted him: *"It hurts to see you going through anything that's not conducive to your family dynamic. I'm here, sweetheart, when you're ready to talk."*

She thought she was being a supportive fiancée, but little did she know it would blow up in her face. When Christopher returned home, he asked Summer for her car keys. This surprised her because she knew he wouldn't be caught dead riding in her car. So, she inquired about his reasoning.

"Baby, why do you need my car keys?" she asked.

"Bobby from the dealership will be by to pick up your vehicle and discuss what type of luxury car you'd be comfortable driving," he said, emphasizing the word "luxury."

"No, Christopher. You know what that car means to me," she said, her eyes welling up with tears.

Christopher instantly flew off the handle, his voice echoing through the house as he screamed and paced in a fit of rage.

"You are a grown ass woman! All this sentimental shit has to stop! The car is being picked up today."

"Christopher, please! Why are you not hearing me? Why would you ask me to get rid of a car Mimi purchased for me? I have nothing of hers. Nothing! Why are you doing this?" Summer cried out.

Christopher was hovering over her while she was seated, yelling.

"No woman... No... No wife of mine will be riding around in a fucken' Kia!"

Summer knew that all this misdirected anger was him taking out his family drama on her. Therefore, she decided it was best to sit quietly, knowing she wouldn't be able to reason with him while he was upset. So, she opted to wait until he had calmed down before revisiting the conversation. Joining Christopher at the dinner table, she tried to make him see her perspective.

"Hey, I understand you want me to upgrade, and I will. I'll just keep my car parked in the garage."

Christopher dropped his fork onto the plate and stared at Summer with a mean and vicious look in his eyes. Then, he spoke in a threatening tone.

"That cheap ass car will not be parked in my garage. I'm done with this conversation. If that car means that much to you, keep it! Leave in it, but bet one damn thing, I won't be marrying you," he said as he walked upstairs.

Summer was shocked. She couldn't believe he could be so heartless, knowing what that car meant to her. As she sat in dismay, she could hear him on the phone with the dealership. Moments later, he came downstairs and asked her what style of Mercedes-Benz SUV she would like. Summer was too angry to answer, so Christopher, in his insensitivity, ordered her an AMG-style Obsidian Black Metallic Mercedes-Benz SUV with black leather interior with red stitching. Ironically, it was the same style and color SUV they were in the first time Christopher hit her.

As he ended the call, he walked out the door and said, "That car better be gone when I return. It's no longer an option."

Summer, fueled by her determination not to lose her car, leaped out of the chair and made her way to Mr. Ben's apartment, an hour's drive across town. After a couple of knocks, he opened the door and greeted her, saying, "Hello, baby girl. I didn't think I'd ever see you again."

Summer explained that Christopher wanted her to upgrade her vehicle and asked if she could leave her car with him for a week. Mr. Ben agreed and then dropped Summer off at the hospital. On the way, she called ahead and asked Ebony to pick her up from the job and take her home. Christopher had called several times, and she refused to answer while in the car with Mr. Ben. She prayed that he wasn't riding around looking for her or, even worse, parked at her job. To be safe, she called him when she entered the hospital.

"Where the fuck are you?!" Christopher screamed.

"I sold the car, baby. I was in with the notary," Summer explained.

"How in the hell have you sold your car in less than three hours? Summer, stop fucken' playing with me!" he yelled.

She explained that she had an aide who worked on her unit and often arrived late because she was a single mom of four with no car. She had worked out a payment agreement with the employee.

"I'd rather see someone who really needs the car end up with it rather than you have someone to destroy it because it's not luxurious enough for you."

Christopher demanded to know her location so he could pick her up. However, she told him that Ebony was bringing her home. He hung up on her just as Ebony pulled up. Ebony looked at Summer, knowing how hurt she must be. She reached over and gave her a comforting hug. Summer cried the entire ride home. She told Ebony that Christopher was not being honest with himself. He was living for his dad's attention in any way he could get it, and she was just collateral damage.

When they pulled into the driveway, Summer sat in the car, afraid to go in. Ebony was also afraid to cross Christopher, so she kept her opinions to herself. Suddenly, the passenger car door opened, and Christopher tugged at Summer's arm.

"Ebony, thank you for bringing her home, but we need to talk. Summer, get out of the car," Christopher demanded.

Summer complied and headed toward the house. She entered the front door first and suddenly felt his hand around the back of her neck. Immediately, she fell to the floor, curled up with her knees to her chest, and tried to cover her face to avoid injuries to her face.

"Get the hell up!" he yelled as he tried to pick her up off the floor.

However, he was unsuccessful because of her position. He threatened to drag her upstairs by her foot if she didn't get up and walk. As he yelled, Summer pleaded with him for mercy. When he tried to pull her feet first up the stairs, she straightened her body and attempted to walk. Then, he began to drag her up the stairs by her hair. She could feel her hair ripping from her scalp as he forcefully pulled her.

Summer screamed out, "What did I do, Christopher? What did I do?"

He threw her onto the bed and walked into the closet. When he pulled a belt from the belt hanger, she realized that he was about to beat her with a belt. She tried to run to the opposite side of the bed, but he swung the belt, and it landed on her upper back and shoulder. The tip of the belt wrapped around and slapped her neck. Summer fell backward out of bed and got pinned between the bed and the wall. She used the blanket to block the belt from hitting her. Christopher yanked her from the side of the bed, and then he pinned his weight on top of her and rolled the belt around his fist. Her arms were pinned down under his knees, exposing her face. He threatened to punch her if she didn't admit what she did with the car and who she was with. Summer kept to her same story as Christopher threatened to bash her face in.

Finally, he released her as she scooted back into the corner. She sat against the wall with her knees pulled up to her chest, terrified.

He paced the room, screaming, "You could have been in an accident or anything! And then you weren't answering my damn call."

Suddenly, he ran back over to her and pulled on her shirt while accusing her of cheating. Summer stayed quiet and still as he sat in the chair next to her. It felt like she was on the floor for eternity. Her body ached, and her leg was beginning to go numb. She was afraid to move. She straightened her fingers, looking at her engagement ring. She contemplated taking it off and making a run for it. But Christopher's voice snapped her into reality.

"If you attempt to remove that ring, I will permanently break your finger to make sure you can never pull it off."

Summer didn't say anything as she stood and walked to the bathroom. He followed her and snatched her pants and underwear off as she attempted to use the restroom. He even sniffed the seat of her underwear as if he really thought she could have been with another man.

However, Summer knew that Christopher didn't believe she was out cheating. The problem was that she clearly defied a command from him, and he wanted to ensure that she knew there were consequences. Too afraid to move, she sat quietly on the toilet as he stepped into the shower. Afterward, she stood before the mirror and washed her hands. She captured a glimpse of herself in the mirror and ran her fingers through her hair. Large patches came out in her hand.

Her eyes filled with tears as she looked over her body for bruises and wondered how to hide the large belt whip that was clearly visible across her neck. It was warm outside, so she'd look crazy in a turtleneck.

Besides the large patches of hair missing, the other bruises were minor. She just needed to hide her neck. As she examined herself, Christopher stepped out of the shower. He felt guilty for his actions as he noticed all her hair in the sink.

"Summer, baby, please don't leave me. I promise I will go to counseling and seek help," he pleaded as he walked up to her and pulled her to him.

"I made you a promise in Bora Bora, and I meant it. I just see red, and my anger consumes me. I don't know how to control it sometimes. Tell me what you want me to do?"

Summer walked off, refusing to be a part of his show. She attempted to sleep on the sofa alone, but he followed her downstairs and hopped on the couch behind her. He held her like nothing had happened.

The following morning, Christopher awakened Summer by informing her that she'd have to drive one of his vehicles to work until they had time to pick her SUV up from the dealership. She wanted nothing to do with him. Still, she got dressed and did as he asked. She grabbed her vision board that outlined the life she wanted with him and threw it in the dumpster outside her job. Then, she entered the building and tried to act normal. She exited the elevator wearing a large bandage on her neck. Ebony followed her to her office and closed the door.

"Summer, if you don't take that 6x6 big ass bandage off your neck, looking like Willie the fool. You are making people stare."

"I hate him, Ebony," Summer cried out. "I'm leaving him and going back home. He will never change.

Summer and Ebony had each other's backs. They devised a pact that if Summer were in danger and needed Ebony's help, she would text two black hearts. They even came up with a secret meeting place. She knew that this life as she knew it was over. The good thing was that the contractors finished all repairs on Miss Dangerfield's home. She called Mr. Jeffery and informed him she was sending her car and furniture back home. Then, she secretly hired a moving company to empty her storage unit and have her furniture and car sent back home.

# CHAPTER 16: DARKNESS

Summer had given up on a happily ever after. She couldn't trust Christopher. On the one hand, he was everything she ever needed, but on the other hand, he was a complete monster. The emotional turmoil within her was unbearable.

Christopher wasn't willing to lose Summer, especially not willing to allow her to be free without him. As she fell back into her typical pattern of going along to get along, she knew how not to rock the boat.

It was time for Summer to step into her new position on the job, a stark contrast to her personal life. Stevin informed her of an out-of-state seminar that was mandatory for her to attend. She'd have to fly out and be in attendance the entire week for the upcoming week.

Summer called Christopher to inform him that she had to go out of town for work and requested that he fly to Texas with her so she wouldn't have to travel alone. Hoping he'd say no, her wish was granted. She was in disbelief that he didn't attempt to sabotage her job. He agreed that she could attend without finding a reason to argue.

Summer planned to enjoy her time away from Christopher the entire week, finding the peace she couldn't receive at home.

Stevin and other staff members also attended the seminar. He made several attempts to get Summer to come out and enjoy Dallas's nightlife after business meetings. However, she didn't trust Christopher, so she kept her distance from Stevin. For all she knew, Christopher could have had her room bugged or could have had her followed.

It was apparent that Stevin wanted more from Summer during the trip. Therefore, she purposely lagged behind after the meetings ended to avoid walking out with him. She also didn't want him to know her hotel room number. Summer spent every available minute on the phone with Christopher, often falling asleep while video chatting with him. He made it seem as if he really missed her and needed to hear her voice and see her face while she was out of town. However, Summer knew it was his way of controlling her from a distance.

*Airport Disaster*

When Summer returned home, Christopher met her inside the airport. To her surprise, he was standing at baggage claim waiting for her. She only traveled with a carry-on bag, so she needed no assistance with her bag. Summer tried to rush out of the airport to avoid Christopher, seeing that most of the recruiters who traveled in her circle were men. She could see Stevin out of the corner of her eye, and it looked as if he were headed in her direction. She was thinking to herself that if he even dared to walk over to her while she was standing next to Christopher, she'd karate chop him in his throat. Her hands began to sweat, and her heart raced as Stevin made a beeline straight to

Christopher. If looks could kill, Stevin would have fallen out at her feet and started to have convulsions while foaming from the mouth. I'll be damned if Stevin didn't walk straight to Christopher, introducing himself while shaking his hand.

"Oh, Summer, you left your laptop charger at the conference table. I meant to give it to you yesterday, but it slipped my mind."

At that moment, Summer sensed Stevin had a hidden agenda. In their three encounters, he had never mentioned her charger. She could see Christopher tensing up as he placed his hand on her lower back. Summer had learned over the years that the strategic hand placement on her lower back was his claim to her. It said, "Don't look or touch." Summer quickly snatched her card.

"Thank you, Stevin," she said as she wrapped her arm around Christopher and walked off.

She knew WWIII was about to occur, so she had to think quickly on her feet.

"So, who was that?" Christopher asked.

"That's Mr. Bash. He's the head of our recruiting department. He's the individual who recruited me into this company." Summer's introduction of Stevin only entices Christopher's interest, leaving him with more questions than answers.

"So, you knew him before moving here?"

"No, baby, he was the first person I met when I arrived. His office is located in the hospital."

"How much contact do you have with him daily?"

"Until a couple of weeks ago, little to none. He only trained me for this position."

"So, you didn't think you needed to tell me you were traveling with another guy, Summer?" Christopher's voice was tinged with suspicion. The tension in the car was thick.

"I didn't travel with him, Christopher. We didn't arrive together."

"Where did he stay? Where was his room?"

"I imagine that all our crew stayed in the same hotel. Now, where his room was located, I don't know. We only saw each other during the conference."
Christopher sat quietly, rubbing his chin. "Did any of your crew hang out?"

"They probably did, but I spent all my free time on the phone with you. So, I'm not sure what they did."

Summer sensed Christopher's unease and knew he wasn't going to let it go. So, she reached over and started rubbing the back of his neck.

"Can I show you how much I missed you?" she asked while rubbing her hand over the crotch of his pants. "Can I show you, Daddy?"

She unzipped his pants, pulled his penis out, and stroked it in an up-and-down motion. She played with it until it was fully erect. Then, she leaned over and submerged his giant cock into her mouth.

"Hold on. You're going to make me wreck," Christopher said but never tried to stop her from pleasuring him.

She used her hands in a grinding motion as she sucked harder. She felt the car swirl, so she looked up while continuing to play with his cock with both hands. Christopher tried to focus on the road as the pleasure overtook him. Summer looked at him with a seductive smile while stroking his penis until he made a large splash. This behavior from her only turned him on more, and Summer knew it. She was willing to do anything to avoid the Stevin interrogation.

He sped into the driveway and quickly parked the car, jumping out and opening Summer's door. When she stepped out, he threw her over his shoulder and entered the house, pinning her against the wall in the foyer; he took all of her right in the entranceway.

Summer drove him even wilder, whispering in his ear how much she loved and missed him and never wanted to leave his side. They had sex from the foyer to the shower, then the bed. Summer pulled out every trick in the book that her mind could think of to keep the Stevin conversation dead. She rode him until he passed out. Then, she rolled over and eased out of bed.

She was exhausted from her trip and the hot, steamy sex. Still, she went downstairs and prepared dinner. She figured if Christopher's belly was full and he was sexually satisfied, there wasn't any room for him to be angry. As she finished dinner and was ready to turn in herself, he eased up behind her, squeezing and rubbing all over her.

"Baby, you were wild today."

"I guess with this being my first time traveling alone, I really miss you and not being able to touch you; all those feelings just built up this week," Summer replied. "I guess I need to go out of town more," she laughed.

Christopher turned her around to face him and softly kissed her lips. "No, sweetie, your traveling alone days are over."

"That's even better," she said, laying her head on his chest and thinking, "I have to get out of this relationship."

He lifted her up and placed her on the countertop to be at eye level with him.

"I want to know more about this Stevin."

"What would you like to know?" she asked as her eyes rolled to the back of her head.

"Is he married?"

"I don't know. I don't think he is."

"Is he dating any women on the job?"

"Now, that I don't know, Christopher. Why are you asking me so many questions about Mr. Bash?"

"I can't ask questions about your boss. Is there something I need to know?

Summer slid down off the counter and walked away.

"I can't believe we can have great moments like today, and you still find a way to make me feel less than," she said as she walked up the stairs. She intentionally fell asleep, praying that that would end that conversation.

## CHAPTER 17: STEVIN IS ON HER BAD SIDE

It was Monday morning, and Christopher had been under Summer since she returned from Texas. She hadn't had a moment to herself to talk to Ebony about Stevin's antics at the airport.

The morning meeting couldn't end fast enough. Ebony sat across the table, trying to keep a straight face and avoid bursting out in laughter as Summer sent her text messages describing what she wanted to do to Stevin - not using any kind words. After the meeting, Ebony joined Summer in her office. Being the character that she is, she was on the floor in tears, laughing as Summer walked her through the events at the airport and the sex tricks that she had to pull out of the bag to keep from coming to work with two black eyes.

While Summer was in character, none other than Stevin showed up to her office. She tried to keep a straight face and remain professional despite wanting to choke the life out of him. He had brought some unnecessary paperwork to her office. However, it was clear that he had his own agenda, which explained his bold behavior at the airport.

Ebony left them alone and closed Summer's office door as she exited. Ten minutes into the meeting, Christopher called. Summer decided that she'd call him back after her meeting with Stevin. He instantly sent her an irate text, so she asked Stevin to give her a moment, and she called him from her office phone. He yelled loudly, his voice vibrating through the phone, asking why she was closed up in her office with Stevin. Keeping a personal persona, she informed him that she was in a meeting with a superior.

Christopher could be heard using vulgar profanity towards Stevin. Summer was mortified; it was obvious that Stevin could hear all or part of her conversation.

As Stevin silently packed up his paperwork and left her office, Summer was at a loss for words. She was unable to talk him down, and the realization struck her that this could be the beginning of the end of her career. She held the phone, feeling the weight of the accusation of sleeping with Stevin. Finally, she hung up on Christopher as he continued to berate her. Confused and shaken, she left her office to search for Ebony, wondering how Christopher had received information about who was in her office.

As she turned the corner, there was Amber sitting at the nurses' station with a sly grin on her face. It took everything in Summer not to whoop her ass. She was outraged that Christopher was even talking to Amber. She even sent a text threatening to leave him because of it.

Summer couldn't believe he was communicating with Amber, and she had no fear of him at that moment. Summer eventually located Ebony and informed her about the situation. Ebony immediately lost it and confronted Amber about her behavior. Their argument got so heated that human resources had to intervene, resulting in Ebony being suspended for three days. This incident marked the end of Amber and Ebony's friendship.

Summer returned to her office and closed the door. Meanwhile, Christopher texted and called throughout the workday, but she didn't reply. When she got home, the tables had turned, and he had to explain why he was communicating with Amber. However, he denied having any communication with her.

They argued throughout the night, and Christopher saw a rage in Summer's eyes that he'd never seen before. He opted to sleep in the guest bedroom and didn't attempt to lay a finger on her. For the first time, he was worried and thought the night could possibly end like the movie "The Burning Bed."

Summer returned to work with a sense of dread, fearing she could be fired at any moment. With Ebony suspended and the Bitch from the Wicked West still at work, the atmosphere was tense. Summer was pretty sure she would be arrested for assault. It had been two days since she had seen Stevin, and she felt the need to apologize to him. She snuck off her unit to visit him in his office, only to be informed that he was on leave. She hurried back to her office and immediately called him on his personal cell number. He told her that he had been temporarily removed from his position because of an investigation. Two nurses had filed a grievance against him, alleging sexual assault, a shocking revelation that left her speechless.

He told her that he believed everything was connected back to her. She told him that she truly believed Amber was behind the false claims. She explained to him that there was a possibility

Christopher and Amber were setting him up. She also told him that Amber was behind the angry call she received from Christopher.

Summer was in disbelief that Christopher would go so far. This was confirmation that she had to plan her escape. She hung up with Stevin and didn't go straight home after work. Instead, she stopped by Ebony's house to inform her about what was happening with Stevin. They stood in the driveway and talked because they didn't want Thomas to hear their conversation.

Summer was trying to figure a way out. She talked to Ebony about the possibility of returning home and taking a position with her old job. As they devised a plan of escape, Christopher pulled up in front of Ebony's residence. They both stared in disbelief. How did he know her location? He sat in the car with the windows up as if he was waiting for Summer to get into the car with him. When he never got out, Summer walked to the car. As she reached for the passenger door, Christopher hit the gas and pulled off, leaving her standing at the end of the driveway. Summer knew he was ready for war. She ended her conversation with Ebony and made the dreaded drive home. When she pulled into the driveway, Christopher was standing in the garage, leaning against his car. Summer parked, and he walked over to her SUV. She lowered her window to talk to him.

"Umm, you had to run and tell your friend that your play toy got fired?"

Summer looked up at Christopher, and her eyes widened in shock. "I knew you and that hungry bitch were behind this; I can't believe you would stoop so low. How could you tarnish his career and reputation out of your own insecurities? Why would you do that?"

"So, when were you going to tell me that you and your boyfriend, Stevin, had something going on before you met me?"

"Christopher, what are you talking about? You just want to find something to fight about."

"So, this man never tried to talk to you?"

"No, he's never tried to talk to me."

"Bitch, you are a liar!" he yelled as he pulled her door open and tried to pull her out of the SUV.

Summer was fed up with the abuse from him, so she grabbed her umbrella from the floorboard and began beating his arm with it. This only made him more enraged. He continued to ask her about Stevin.

"I already know he tried to talk to you, so stop lying."

By now, he was standing over her with his fists balled up, screaming, "So he never tried to talk to you? I already know Ebony tried to hook you guys up."

At that moment, she knew without a doubt that Amber had her hand in this. Summer was fed up with him screaming.

"If you want to listen to your girlfriend's lies, go right ahead. I hope you screwing her also because you will never touch me again. So, go call and tell her that."

"I'm not talking to that damn woman. This is not about her!" Christopher yelled.

He could see Summer wasn't backing down, but he knew that if he hit her, this could very well push her completely out of his life. So, he jumped in his car and sped away.

No matter how angry Christopher was at Summer, in his warped mind, it was important for her to know that he was loyal to her. Knowing how Summer felt about Amber, he had to pick his battle, and the thought that Stevin had been fired was good enough for him.

Summer went inside and locked herself in one of the downstairs bedrooms and placed a chair behind the door so Christopher couldn't get in. When he returned home, he realized that Summer was locked behind the closed bedroom door.

Christopher attempted to pick the lock but couldn't get in because the chair was propped under the doorknob, keeping it secure. He started tapping on the door, begging Summer to open up and come out and talk to him.

"Summer, I'm not communicating with Amber, and I'm not cheating on you. I didn't have anything to do with that dude losing his job. I admit I called and checked up on you, but I never conversed directly with Amber. None of what's happening at your job had anything to do with me. I promise, baby."

Summer was certain that Christopher was lying through his teeth. He was just more concerned with getting back that submissive, quiet, shy woman who hung on to every word he spoke.

Eventually, he realized that she was not going to come out of the locked bedroom, so he left her alone. Summer was surprised by Christopher's response to her defying him. She was scared to leave the bedroom the next morning, but to her surprise, Christopher was up before her preparing breakfast. He took her by the hand and sat her on the sofa. Then, he spent the morning apologizing and denying having any relationship with Amber.

# CHAPTER 18: MY BAE IS BACK

Summer went to work excited because it was the day that Ebony returned. They spent the rest of the week making Amber's life hell. Ebony was the link to all of her friendships on the job. Most of the staff only tolerated her because of Ebony. Amber would have never imagined that Ebony would use all her deep secrets against her, but all bets were off when it came to Summer. After informing some of the nurses how Amber truly felt about them and her hoeish behavior with some of their significant others, the nurses ran Amber off of the unit by tormenting her. The impact of this torment was so severe that Amber was eventually forced to transfer to an entirely different floor of the hospital, a move that deeply affected her ego.

Summer was thrilled that she no longer had to see Amber's face daily. She had also changed position and would move to her new office on a different floor. Her new position brought a significant change in her work routine, as she didn't have to be on the job site for eight hours; she mostly worked from home and even visited Mr. Ben some days to avoid being home with Christopher.

Stevin never returned to Glendale Hospital. However, it was rumored that all claims against him were suddenly dropped. He transferred to another hospital in a different state. Summer was too afraid to call him to see how he was doing. She was happy just knowing Christopher didn't cost him his entire career.

## What Wedding

Summer decided to work from home one day. While sitting in the office, she could hear Christopher rambling throughout the house.

"Summer! Where is all the wedding planning information? I don't see your book or vision board. What have you been doing? I have no details about my own wedding."

Summer was speechless because she had trashed those items months ago.

Christopher's frustration boiled over, "Say something, Summer!" As she sat with a blank look on her face, he said, "Fuck it! I'll just hire a wedding planner myself. That's the best thing to do anyway."

He then sat in the office with her and made several calls to schedule a meeting with a wedding planner. Summer gave little input.

"What is the wedding date?" he asked.

"We never set a specific date," Summer replied. Christopher looked at her with rage in his eyes as he ended the call.

"Do you not want to marry me anymore?" he asked. "No... No, don't even answer that. I won't play these games.

We meet with the wedding planner on Friday. You better have a date before the meeting, and that's all I have to say about that."

Throughout the day, Summer received multiple calls from a California area code. Not knowing the number, she refused to answer. Later that evening, while she and Christopher were snuggling and watching a movie, her phone rang again from an unknown number. Summer looked at the phone and placed it down, ignoring the call.

"Who is that?" Christopher asked.

"I don't know," she said as he snatched her phone.

"I don't know who's calling. That number has been calling me all week, but I have no idea who it is.

Christopher demanded her to unlock the phone. When he opened it to the call log, he immediately jumped off the sofa and walked out into the garage. Summer was curious about what was going on, so she attempted to check on him. As she approached the kitchen, she could hear him yelling.

"I will do it in my own damn time! It's my fucking life!"

Summer tried to open the door to the garage, but he forcefully pushed her back into the house and slammed the door.

She stood at the door, eavesdropping. From the conversation, she gathered that Christopher was talking to his father. His father was the one who had been calling her phone. She was puzzled about why he would be calling her and knew it wouldn't end well. The mystery of his interest in her deepened her sense of impending trouble.

 Christopher stormed back inside, visibly upset. He knocked everything off the counter, startling Summer. Paralyzed with fear and unable to move, she was scared to ask questions. She pressed against the wall, praying that he didn't turn his rage on her.

Christopher's voice reverberated through the house, filled with a mix of anger and desperation. "He can't just let me live! Why can't he stay the fuck out of my life?" He strode over to Summer, his eyes blazing, forbidding her to answer his dad's calls. "Do you hear me, Summer? You better never speak with him outside my presence."

He was yelling and using hand gestures as if he'd smack her if she disobeyed. Then, he left without explaining what had just happened. All Summer could do was feel empathy for Christopher. She couldn't understand why his father was so hard on him.

She was in bed when he returned home. He walked into the bedroom and sat on the edge of the bed. Summer hugged him from behind. He grabbed her and pulled her to his lap. She sat with her arm around his neck as she grabbed his face, kissed him, and told him she loved him. Despite all the turmoil, it broke her heart to see him hurt and vulnerable.

"Summer, I know I've made mistakes, but everything I have done is because I love you and can't bear the thought of losing you. I'm sorry for anything I've ever done that's made you doubt my love for you. You're my world. I would die if you weren't part of my life. I can't imagine life without you."

Summer held Christopher tightly; nothing mattered more than prioritizing his peace of mind above all else. That evening, he slept tightly clutching Summer, as if he feared losing her at any moment.

\*\*\*

When Christopher returned home from work the next day, he walked into the bedroom in a sour mood and told her she needed to take some time off work because they would be flying out to California to meet with his family. Summer didn't want to upset him any further, so she just agreed without asking any questions. She waited until he looked relaxed before asking which days she needed to get covered for work. He told her to take the entire next week off.

Summer felt it would be impossible to take off so many days with such short notice.

"Christopher, I can't just request an entire week off with such little notice."

Christopher didn't acknowledge her, so she decided she'd have to call out sick and make an unnecessary trip to urgent care to get the days covered. Summer was still afraid to rock the boat and ask any questions related to his dad, knowing Christopher's anger was unpredictable when it came to his father; he was a ticking time bomb. Besides, they had a meeting with the wedding planner the next day and that was enough stress within itself. She still had apprehensions about marrying him.

The next morning, Summer made sure to work from the office. Throughout the day, she received several texts from Christopher reminding her about today's meeting with the wedding planner. When the meeting time approached, she took a break and met him at the wedding planner's office. She dreaded talking with a wedding planner and needed to see significant changes from Christopher before she could proceed with the wedding.

The meeting was pleasant, and they seemed to have an idea of which direction they'd take with the plans. After the meeting, they went their separate ways, and Summer headed back to the office. Summer called Ebony from the car.

"Hello," Ebony answered.

"I'm fucked."

"What happened?"

"Nothing bad happened. Everything was perfect, but I'm so confused, Ebony. Christopher was so excited. I have never seen him not in control of his feelings and this excited about something in public. This man was like a kid in a candy shop. His eyes were lit up like a Christmas tree. The plans for the wedding are so beautiful. He truly wants this. What am I supposed to do with all these emotions?"

"Follow your heart, friend," Ebony said, holding back her true feelings.

Summer ended the call by setting up a lunch date with Ebony. She told her that she needed to see her before her trip on Monday. Later that evening, Summer returned home walking on rose petals. Christopher had sprinkled them along with tealight candles throughout the home.

They enjoyed a candlelight dinner and slow danced throughout the night. Meeting with the wedding planner and actually having a wedding date brought out the happy and grateful Christopher that she first fell in love with.

*The Dreaded Meeting*

Summer was in need of some girl time, so she and Ebony met for lunch. Halfway through their meal, she received a frantic call from Christopher, demanding that she come home immediately. His father had sent his private jet demanding their presence. Confused and worried, Summer told Ebony that something was wrong and that she would call her as soon as she could.

When Summer arrived home, she was shocked to see the personal driver loading packed luggage, even though she hadn't packed anything herself. Christopher wouldn't let her enter the house and directed her to the car. They were off to the airport without any explanation.

Christopher remained silent, nervously fidgeting. His leg shook, and he rubbed his sweaty hands back and forth on his pants. Summer sensed that something significant was imminent. As they boarded the private jet, Christopher remained on the phone the entire time. Summer overheard him speaking with his mother, asking her to intervene on his behalf. He also talked with his father, requesting to meet at a restaurant instead of the family home. He informed his dad that he didn't give him much of an option but to fly out and see him, requesting they meet the following day.

"Can we do this tomorrow? Summer needs to rest."

Summer finally worked up enough nerves to ask Christopher what was going on. However, he was not being forthcoming. He told her that his father wanted to destroy him. He asked that she just stick by his side and not let his father divide them. Christopher kissed her on the forehead and held her tight. When they checked into the hotel, he left Summer and went straight to his parents' home. When she went through her bag, she noticed that he had packed lightly for her, and she was missing all the necessary essentials. Christopher had not packed her birth control, and she had forgotten to take them this morning. She tried to reach him on his cell, but he didn't answer.

Summer was fine with staying at the hotel as she had no interest in meeting with his family. She was already dreading the upcoming meet and greet, so she never questioned why he wanted to go alone. When Christopher returned to the hotel suite, she could tell he had been crying. He laid on top of her, burying his face in her chest. She lifted his head and said. "Talk to me, baby."

He very aggressively kissed her and then pulled her down, bringing her body completely under his. He firmly caressed his hand all over her body. Summer attempted to stop him and told him that she hadn't taken her birth control, and he didn't pack it. Christopher ignored her as he continued to aggressively have sex with her as if he were releasing all his frustration out through extremely rough sex.

The following day, Christopher walked around the spacious, dimly lit room, pacing back and forth.

"Baby, why are we doing this if it has you this upset?"

He grabbed her and pinned her down on the bed. Then, he made love to her like this would be their last moments together. Christopher held Summer in his arms until it was time to get dressed and meet his parents. Summer asked Christopher to stop by the pharmacy to pick up a Plan B emergency contraceptive pill to prevent pregnancy.

Although she wanted to have kids in the future, she didn't want to become pregnant under the current circumstances. Christopher agreed, and they obtained the pill. Summer removed the pill from its box, keeping the pill sealed in the foil wrapping. She stuck it in her purse to take it later during dinner. They exited the car and walked into a private room in the restaurant. Christopher's mother greeted Summer first with a big hug.

"Aren't you a cute little thing!" his mother said.

Christopher's brothers stood to greet Summer as his father remained seated. She simply shook his hand. Christopher sat with his elbows on the table, his hands pressed to his face as if he were praying.

"Remove your elbows from the table, son," his father requested.

Christopher sat back in his chair as if it was doomsday.

His dad turned to Summer and asked, "How are you, young lady? Are you excited about the upcoming nuptials?"

"Yes, sir," she answered. "Christopher has been great with helping me plan our big day," she said as she grabbed his hand. He held her hand tightly and kissed the back of it.

"So, Summer, tell me a little about yourself," Mr. Diamond continued.

Summer gave him vague responses, not wanting to go too deep into her past.

"Well, Christopher has updated me that you recently lost your closest family member. What family will you have at the wedding?" His father's question was direct, almost probing.

"Dad!" Christopher's voice cracked with frustration. "You already know the answer to that question. Why are you doing this?"

"Calm down, son. I'm just getting to know Summer. Let her respond to me, please!" His father's voice was calm, but there was a hint of concern in his eyes.

"Mr. Diamond, I don't have any family. However, I have met wonderful neighbors and coworkers that will be in attendance."

"Do you know your parents, Summer?"

"No, sir, I do not."

"Have you ever looked for them?"

"No, sir, I haven't," she said as she dropped her head.

"Why is this? Do you not want to know, or has the opportunity never presented itself to do the research?"

"I have always been told that the state never had any information on who my parents were."

"So, you never wondered how you got the last name Taylor? Did you ever research yourself? Is it that you don't want to know?"

Summer started to tear up, feeling judged. She shook her head and responded in a soft, squeaky voice. "I don't know what to do. I was always told there weren't any records."

"Would you want to know if you had the power and resources?"

"Yes. I guess I just gave up a long time ago."

Christopher jumped up from the table, screaming loudly in the restaurant and making a scene.

"Why are you doing this, Dad? Leave her alone. You already know the answers to all these damn questions."

Christopher's brother grabbed him by the arm, trying to get him to calm down. As they attempted to lead him outside, Christopher only became more furious, screaming for Summer to leave with him.

Mr. Diamond's authoritative voice cut through the chaos, ordering Summer to remain at the table, instructing Christopher's two older brothers to take him outside and calm him down.

However, Christopher's rage only escalated, becoming more violent. Summer, feeling the tension, apologized and informed Mr. Diamond that she needed to step out and check on Christopher.

"Wait, young lady. I need to talk to you."

Christopher's mother told his father to let Summer go and calm him down. She was embarrassed by the scene he was causing in the upscale restaurant.

Summer walked outside to find Christopher almost in blows with his brothers. She stepped between them, and Christopher wasted no time snatching her up by the arm and putting her in the car. He had the driver to hightail out the parking lot.

Summer couldn't get a single word in. Christopher was booking airline tickets on the first flight out of California. When they arrived at the hotel, he stayed in the car, talking on the phone. He ordered Summer to go up to the room, pack their bags, and then come back down. He also made her leave her phone in the car.

Summer followed his orders and packed as quickly as she could. In her heart, something was definitely off. It was clear that Christopher was keeping something from her, but she was too afraid to ask. When she returned to the car, they headed straight to the airport. As they boarded the plane, Summer learned he had booked their flights to Atlanta, Georgia. Summer was confused about why he hadn't booked them to return home. As always, she didn't push the issue; she just waited until they were settled in the hotel before she demanded an explanation.

Christopher confided in her, revealing his father's apprehension towards their union. His father feared the unknown, particularly of her family, and his nervousness about the potential impact on his company and reputation was the reason behind his opposition.

"I won't let them treat you like this, Summer. I just won't! I don't want to hurt your feelings, but I had to be truthful with you. My father will show up at our home.

I know he will. But I won't let that stop us. I just need time to think. Would you be upset if we fly back to Bora Bora and get married - just the two of us?"

"Christopher, I don't want you to make any decisions out of fear or anger. Let's just wait a week or two before making any big decisions."

After Summer stepped into the bathroom to shower, she could hear Christopher stepping onto the balcony. She waited until he was outside and slowly cracked the bathroom door. It was clear that he was on the phone with his father. She could hear him telling his father that he was in Atlanta handling it himself. Christopher threatened his father, saying that he and Summer would disappear forever if he pulled another stunt like that. Summer started to understand why he was so distant from his father. She didn't take it personally that he was skeptical about their relationship. She understood that his dad had a brand to protect.

Christopher kept her in Atlanta for the next three days. They didn't leave the hotel room. His sex drive had increased times ten.

Finally, the time came for them to leave. Summer was happy to return home. She was thankful that her time of the month was in a couple of days. She could do without sex for the next month, but as she unpacked their bags, she came across the small handbag she carried the night of the dinner. She sat it on the nightstand, and it fell over, spilling its contents on the floor, including the foil wrapping of the Plan B pill. Summer picked up the foil wrapping and realized the pill was still in the wrapping. She had forgotten to take the pill. She had spent the past five days having nonstop unprotected sex with Christopher while off her birth control. She quickly swallowed the pill and sat on the side of the bed with a sickening feeling. With everything happening with Christopher and his father, she knew this was not the time to get pregnant.

# CHAPTER 19: EVERYTHING IS NOT WHAT IT SEEMS

Four days had passed, and Summer realized that her menstrual cycle should have started two days ago. Christopher was still on edge for reasons unknown to her. For this reason, she couldn't dare tell him about her mistake with the emergency contraception.

Summer worked from the office daily, craving the break it offered her, as she needed her space and a break from Christopher and his daddy issues. He had even gone as far as getting her a new phone and changing her number to ensure that his father would have no contact with her, a move that only added to her mental exhaustion.

Christopher was persistent in his desire for a destination wedding, pushing more and more for it to happen sooner rather than later, adding to the pressure Summer was already feeling. Summer eventually gave in to the idea, asking if Ebony and Thomas could fly out with them to be their matron of honor and best man. Christopher agreed, so now she just needed to get Ebony to convince her husband.

Summer was absolutely certain Ebony would be delighted to stand beside her, but getting her husband on board would be challenging.

Thomas had little to no outside communication with Christopher, and the little interaction they did have was forced due to Thomas's fear of threats to bankrupt his company.

Summer was pretty sure he hated Christopher. So, she put a spin on it, presenting it as a free trip to Bora Bora. However, Ebony wasn't sold on the free trip. She had seen enough of Christopher's damaging behavior and wanted no part of Summer to be forever tied to him. Not wanting to hurt her friend's feelings, she put the conversation off by telling her that Thomas hadn't agreed to go yet.

Another week had passed, and Summer hadn't gotten her period. She started back taking her birth control, feeling anxious about the situation. She scheduled an appointment with her gynecologist to have bloodwork done to check her hCG levels. After waiting a week for her appointment, the doctor's office called and pushed her appointment back two more days later. Summer's nerves were on edge. By now, her period was already fourteen days late, and she was pretty sure that she was pregnant. She was so anxious that she asked Ebony to take off work to go with her to the doctor's appointment when the day finally arrived, seeking her much-needed support.

Sitting in the exam room, Summer felt like she was on a rollercoaster of emotions. The doctor walked in and confirmed that she was indeed pregnant. Overwhelmed with fear of Christopher's reaction, Summer broke down. No matter how much she wanted this for them one day, she knew it was not the right time. She requested the doctor terminate the pregnancy. However, the doctor refused, citing, 'I have a religious objection to doing so.' Unless the pregnancy posed a threat to Summer, she would have to go into an abortion clinic. Summer put off calling the clinic for two weeks. Days later, while sitting at her desk, trying to muster up the courage to tell Christopher, she finally found the right words and the courage to do so. Suddenly, her office phone rang, and it was none other than Christopher's mom calling.

She started the conversation by asking how their trip to Atlanta went. Summer answered, explaining that the entire trip was bittersweet, and she hated that their meeting ended like it did. Mrs. Diamond told her that it was a joy meeting her. She said that she loved Christopher and didn't want him to marry without his family being by his side. She pleaded with Summer to have Christopher call her. Summer, with a determined tone, ended the call, promising her that she would do everything in her power to have him reach out to her.

When she got home from work, Christopher was in the bedroom going through boxes in the master walk-in closet. Summer sat on the bed.

"Christopher, your mother called my work phone today."

When he didn't respond, she attempted to enter the closet, thinking Christopher could not hear her. However, he'd heard every word she spoke and was frozen in fear about Summer's conversation with his mom.

"Come again," he said as he walked out of the closet.

"Your mother called my office phone today pleading with me to have you call her."

"What else did she say?" Christopher asked in a harsh tone.

"Nothing, Christopher. She asked about our Atlanta trip, and I just said the entire trip was bittersweet."

His entire body language changed. "What the fuck else was said, Summer?"

"Nothing, Christopher. Just call her."

Before Summer could finish her statement, Christopher had backhanded her across her face. He struck her with so much force that her feet left the floor, and she fell back on the bed. She immediately felt like her face was glass, and Christopher had just shattered it into a million tiny pieces. She was pretty sure that he had broken her nose.

Summer was lying on the bed choking on her own blood as it pooled in the back of her throat. She was gasping for breath, feeling like he had knocked the wind out of her. He stormed off in a rage after punching a large hole in the wall.

"Why can't they just leave us the fuck alone? I told you not to talk to them, Summer!" he screamed as he walked downstairs.

Summer could hear him on the phone arguing with someone. Still in shock, she attempted to stand. She couldn't stop the nosebleed. She fell back to the bed as she tried to walk to the bathroom for a towel. She was dazed with a pounding headache. With each attempt to stand, she became lightheaded and had double vision. She slid to the floor, crawled to the bathroom, and pulled a towel off the rack. She sat on the floor with the waste basket between her legs as she gagged on her own blood. While holding pressure on her nose until the bleeding stopped, Summer curled up in the fetal position on the bathroom floor, crying hysterically.

She held her stomach, knowing what she had to do. There was no way she could tell Christopher that she was pregnant. Furthermore, there was no way she would marry him. Enough was enough! She wasn't willing to be his human punching bag any longer. She lay on the bathroom floor, crying her eyes out and replaying what she could have done wrong.

Meanwhile, Christopher had calmed down after speaking with his mother. When he returned to the bedroom and saw the bloody mess he had caused, he rushed to the bathroom and found Summer lying on the floor, covered in blood from her severe nosebleed. He ran over to her side.

"Baby, I'm sorry. I never meant to hurt you. I'm just trying to protect you," he said, picking her up off the floor and carrying her to the bed. Then, he ran back into the bathroom to get a wet facecloth and tried to clean her face up.

"Summer, please just talk to me," Christopher repeated as she lay in bed weeping, looking dazed and confused. She turned away from him and balled up as her moans of pain, hurt, and disappointment got louder. He forced himself on top of her and pinned her arms above her head to force her to look into his eyes. Summer laid there with her body limp with a blank stare of emptiness as tears poured from her eyes.

"Baby, we are going to get married, and everything will be okay. I promise everything will be okay once you are my wife. I will never hurt you again, baby. I promise I will never hurt you again."

Christopher got no reaction from her. He just sat there feeling as if he had finally pushed her to a point of no return. He looked at her swollen face, noticing that both of her eyes had begun to turn purple. Throwing his body onto hers, he broke down, bawling with his face buried in her chest.

"I'm done! I have lost you. All I wanted to do was protect you, but I hurt you more than anybody in your life has. I'm going to kill myself!" he screamed as he cried out louder. "I don't want to live any longer if I don't have you by my side."

Summer found it hard to completely detach from him despite all the pain he had caused her. She started to feel pity and sorrow for the very same person who caused her so much physical and mental anguish. She reached up and rubbed the back of his head, trying to calm him down.

Christopher knew the moment she showed him sympathy; she was reeled back in. He placed his arms around her and buried his face in her side. They lay for hours before she asked him to take her to urgent care. However, he was gripped by fear for her to go, and he surely wasn't taking her. He allowed Ebony to come over and take her.

Christopher called Ebony himself and told her that he was having issues with his family. His brother showed up at the house, and they fought. Summer attempted to break up the scuffle, but she got accidentally punched in the face.

Summer didn't murmur a word while riding in the passenger seat of Ebony's car. She never confirmed or denied if his story was true. That was the same story she told the ER doctor, who confirmed that he had indeed broken her nose. When she got home, Summer was so sedated from the pain medication that Christopher had to physically pick her up out of the car and carry her into the house. He then undressed her and put her to bed.

Summer awoke at noon the next day, her head throbbing with pain. She stumbled to the bathroom and faced her reflection in the mirror. The sight of her swollen face, nose splint, and raccoon eyes was a testament to the brutality she had endured from Christopher; it was a crushing blow. Tears streamed down her cheeks, and she was so swollen and bruised that she could hardly recognize herself. Despite her disfigured appearance, she mustered the strength to dress and head to the office.

When she walked downstairs, she found Christopher watching television. She sat directly in front of him with her car keys clutched tightly in her hands.

"Why did you do this to me?"

Christopher hung his head, a silent admission of guilt. He reached out to grab her hand, but she pulled away, her eyes burning with anger. She repeated her question, her voice trembling with emotion.

"How could you do this to me?"

Christopher refused to answer, so Summer jumped up and started walking towards the door.

"Where are you going, Summer?"

"I'm going to work!" she screamed.

"Like hell you are. Why would you go out looking like that?"

Summer, her eyes filled with tears, looked at him with a confused stare and said, "Ask yourself why you would ever put me in a situation where this is the outcome."

She walked out the door, her steps echoing her defiance, and slammed it shut.

While driving to work, she called the abortion clinic and set up an appointment in one week to start the procedures to terminate the pregnancy. Then, she entered her workplace with a clear purpose, not bothering to conceal her injuries. She went straight to HR and requested a medical leave from work. After that, she immediately set out to find Ebony. Summer boldly walked onto the unit, her bruised eyes scanning the unit. When she finally spotted her, she made a beeline for her, determined to seek the support she needed to escape him.

The two of them quickly disappeared into the conference room, where Ebony, shocked by Summer's appearance, hugged her in disbelief.

"Summer, what really happened?" Ebony cried out.

"You already know nothing about my face was an accident," Summer said as her entire body shook from anger.

She told Ebony of her plans to terminate the pregnancy and asked if she would drive her. Ebony agreed, and then Summer left work. She went home and never told Christopher that she had taken a leave of absence from work.

In his typical behavior, he had called in his staff to prepare dinner and clean the house while she was out. That was his attempt to impress her and get back in her goodwill. Summer went upstairs, packed up some items from the master bedroom, and moved into the downstairs bedroom. Then, she locked herself into the bedroom and lay staring at the wall, praying for forgiveness as she prepared herself to snatch life from her body literally.

Christopher, his heart racing, searched throughout the home for Summer. He entered the master bedroom and noticed that she had taken multiple personal items and clothing from their bedroom. Fear gripped him; the thought she might leave him became more real.

Finally, he located her in the guest bedroom downstairs. He turned on the doorknob only to find it was locked. His voice rose in desperation as he began banging on the door, demanding that Summer open it. However, she refused to open it or even address Christopher's demands. In a fit of rage, he kicked the door off the hinges. He stormed into the room, his mind going mad while searching for her suitcase. He found all her clothing packed away in the drawers in the guest bedroom.

Summer was petrified as she sat silently while he gathered all her items and threw everything on their bedroom floor. After emptying out the guest room of all her belongings, he storms back into the room, demanding that Summer get out of the guest bed and return to their bed. She saw the rage in his eyes, so she quickly ran upstairs and picked her items up off the floor, placing them back in the original drawers. Christopher sat in the chair, watching her. Then, he suddenly jumped up and walked towards her. His anger seemed to dissipate, replaced by a deep sadness. Her first reaction was to drop to the floor and curl up for cover. Christopher sat on the floor next to her, looking at her with tears in his eyes as he stroked her face.

"Let's just move away. I promise, if you take me out of this toxic environment with my family, I can be the man you need me to be."

Summer wasn't falling for that. She thought to herself that he was already in self-destruction prior to the fallout with his parents. Like many times before, she was forced to be wrapped in Christopher's arm as he held on to her tightly. She laid awake all night planning her escape.

# CHAPTER 20: GOODBYE BABY

It was the day before her procedure, and Summer's heart was heavy. She had spent a week with frozen peas across her face, and the bruises on her eyes looked like fresh shiners. Christopher was still unaware that she had taken a leave from work. He was out taking meetings for a new project he was managing when the doorbell rang. Without checking the security cameras, Summer opened the door.

There stood Christopher's oldest brother and his mother. Summer knew she was doomed; there was no way she was denying his mother entrance into their home. So, she invited them in, her heart pounding with the fear of Christopher's rage that she knew she'd have to deal with later. Mrs. Diamond touched Summer's face as she was in disbelief. She begged for Summer to tell her that her face wasn't the handiwork of her son.

Summer dropped her head, refusing to cover for him. Mrs. Diamond gasped and grabbed her mouth with tears in her eyes as she stood rubbing Summer's face in disbelief. Summer felt the need to inform Christopher. She mentioned that she needed to call him because he'd be upset if she didn't. When he heard the news that his family was at his home alone with her, he was outraged and insisted that she didn't hang up the phone. He said that he was ten minutes away.

"Why would you let them in?" he screamed, his voice echoing through the phone. Summer held the phone, her apologies a feeble attempt to calm the storm.

They could hear Christopher's car before they saw it as he sped up the driveway. He burst through the front door, looking like Jack Nichols from a scene in The Shining. Summer eased down on the sofa, her heart racing, wondering what part of her face he would break today.

He walked in yelling, "Mother, why are you here?"

"I've come to make it right, son. I won't lose you; I just won't. And why would you do that to Summer's face?"

"It was an accident, Mom. What did you tell her, Summer?" His voice was strained, as if he was trying to convince himself as much as his mother.

"I didn't say anything," she replied in a low voice.

"Go to Ebony's house," he demanded.

"No," his oldest brother interrupted, his voice a mix of authority and concern. "Mom wants to speak with both of you guys. We need to sort this out as a family."

"Get the hell out of my house, Jared," Christopher replied.

"Son, I'm just here to give you, my blessing. I'd love to be a part of the wedding plans. Please don't shut me out."

Christopher paced back and forth, his nervous energy clearly showing he was hiding something. All Summer cared about was the meeting going well, so she didn't have to suffer the backlash. She walked up to Christopher, grabbed him by the hand, and made him sit beside her while addressing his mom.

"Yes, ma'am. I would be delighted to have your motherly input," Summer said as she smiled.

"We are planning to be married in the summer. If you'd like, I can show you our wedding details so far."

Christopher chimed in. "No, not today. I need to talk with my family. Can you please go to Ebony's?

"No, she doesn't have to leave. We're on our way to the hotel. I hope you both can join me for lunch tomorrow. I only came to show you that Mom loves you, sweetheart."

Christopher walked his family out. Summer purposely stood behind the sofa, waiting for his return. They'd have to play tag today. There'd be no off-guard sucker punch if she could help it. Christopher returned and headed straight upstairs, avoiding any conversation with her.

That was just fine with her. Her appointment was at 9:00 a.m. There was no way she could meet them for lunch. Summer entered the bedroom and informed Christopher that she had back-to-back meetings at the office and that she couldn't meet them for lunch the next day.

With a slight pause, Christopher looked up at Summer and said, "You know, sometimes you deserve everything that happens to you," as he walked out of the bedroom. That night, Summer slept with one eye open.

The next morning, she woke up extremely emotional, torn between the rational decision in her head that this was the correct decision, but her heart was overwhelmed with grief. She met Ebony in the parking lot, leaving her SUV at her assigned parking place at work. Ebony had to hold her hand through every step of the process. Summer had to watch a video of the procedure and had to have an ultrasound. She couldn't stomach the video and was so emotional throughout the exam. Ebony never left her side. Then, it happened. There it was - her little pea-sized nugget with a heartbeat.

Motherly emotions flooded Summer's heart. There was no way possible that she could go through the process of terminating her pregnancy. She requested a printout of the ultrasound image and then canceled her upcoming procedure.

"I can't do it, Ebony. I'm a mom," she said with a smile and joyful tears in her eyes, her voice trembling with the weight of her words.

When she returned to Ebony's car, Summer realized that she was so nervous that she had left her phone on the charger in the car. Christopher had called seventy-five times. She had so many text messages that she didn't attempt to read them. When she called Christopher back, she said that she was in a meeting and had left her phone in her office. He didn't let her get another word in as he informed her that she was a damn lie; he had been on her job and learned that she hadn't been to work in weeks because she was out on FMLA.

Christopher yelled, "Summer, your fucken' car is parked in the parking garage. Where the fuck are you? Are you with my family?"

"No, baby, please calm down. I will tell you the truth when I get home; I promise it's not what you're thinking."

"Tell me where you are!"

"I'm picking my car up. I will be home in fifteen minutes. Please, if you don't calm down and let me tell you what's going on, I will not come home."

Christopher paused and then responded in a calmer voice. "Come home. You have left me scared shitless for three damn hours. You are not in a position to be barking orders."

"Ebony is dropping me off at my car now. I promise I'm on my way," Summer said before hanging up.

Ebony chimed in, "No, Summer. He's going to kill you. I won't let you go home alone."

"I'll be okay. I'm going to tell him the truth."

"I can't let you do this," Ebony said as she cried and pleaded with Summer to come home with her and tell Christopher the news over the phone.

Summer started to read Christopher's text messages. Many of the texts said, "I know you are with them," referring to his family.

Ebony voice trembled as she said, "There's something serious going on between him and his family. It's clear there's something he is hiding from you."

Summer disregarded Ebony's concerns, quickly jumped in her car, and headed home. She called Christopher and told him that she had something important to tell him, but he had to be willing to listen.

When she pulled in, he was pacing the driveway. He walked to her car and tugged on the door. Summer's voice cracked as she pleaded with him to hear her out.

"I will be honest with you, but I need you to keep your hands to yourself and listen to me."

"Have you been out cheating on me?" he said with a puzzled face.

"Hell no! Really!?" Summer said, with an annoying tone and expression.

"Unlock the car door."

"No. I won't until you agree to just hear me out. No, I haven't cheated. No, I'm not leaving you. I have news, but it's not what you think."

Christopher stepped back and relaxed his face. She unlocked the door and slowly eased out of the car, grabbing her purse with the paperwork in it and clutching it under her arm. He allowed her to walk into the house. He snatched her purse when he noticed how tightly she clenched onto her purse. Summer used all her might and wrestled with him over the purse. He pushed her to the floor and ran upstairs into the main bedroom, dumping her purse out on the bed.

"No! Please let me explain. I need to explain it to you."

When she entered the bedroom, Christopher stood with a stunned look on his face, holding the sonogram photo.

"Please just hear me out first," she begged.

She recalled the events of her missing the Plan B pill.

"What the hell are you saying? I watched you open the box."

"I was going to take the pill when we got to the restaurant. I removed it from the box and placed the smaller foil package containing the pill in my purse. When everything happened with your family, it completely slipped my mind. I truly had forgotten with everything that was going on, but when I realized what had happened, I took the pill and immediately started my birth control back. Baby, I promise it was a mistake."

"Wait, so this means you've been pregnant for weeks and chose to keep it a secret?"

"I've known three weeks. The only reason I didn't tell you is because I was planning to terminate the pregnancy. Here, look at the paperwork. That's where I've been all morning."

He picked up the paper and read it. "So, is it done?" he asked.

"I couldn't go through with it. I saw our baby on the screen with its little heartbeat. Christopher, it's our baby, and I can't do it."

"So, you tricked me into fatherhood after that being the one thing I asked you not to do. You see everything I'm going through with my family, and you couldn't be true to that one damn thing."

"No, baby, I promise, I was shocked as you are. I won't be angry if you walk away and want nothing to do with the child. I will raise it by myself, and I won't ask you for anything. I promise, Christopher."

Summer's voice was desperate, pleading for his understanding.

"Let me get this straight... You are choosing this baby over me?" Christopher was filled with hurt and disbelief, his eyes searching hers for any sign of regret.

"No, I tried to terminate it, but I can't. I want my baby; it's our child, and it was made from love; it's not a mistake."

Christopher walked over to Summer, gently kissing her forehead. She smiled and relaxed, placing her hands on his chest as she breathed a sigh of relief. Suddenly, with all his might, he balled his fists up and punched her in the abdomen. She dropped to her knees in pain.

He said, "I want you, not that damn thing in your stomach."

Summer was bent over in pain, still clenching onto Christopher, when he pushed her off him and stepped over her. He left her balled up in severe pain, lying on the bedroom floor. He even took her cell phone so she couldn't call for help. Summer knew the pregnancy was over. The power of his punch caused her to start having severe abdominal and lower back pain immediately. She just balled up on the floor, crying and praying for God to protect her baby as she rocked in pain. She laid there for two hours, hoping the cramping would stop, but the pain only got worse. Summer began to feel moist between her legs, so she reached into her underwear and felt wetness on her fingertips. When she looked at her hand, it was covered in blood. She was scared to be alone, so she called out for Christopher. However, he didn't reply. Suddenly feeling sharp back pain and some pressure, Summer walked to the bathroom with blood running down her legs.

"Christopher, please!" she screamed out in pain and grief.

She pulled her clothes down and sat on the toilet as she passed a small clot. A cry of sorrow escaped her lips when she heard a tiny splash hit the water. *She screamed for an hour as if her lost words were finally found and singing her sorrows.* She managed to crawl into the tub with great effort, where she remained for the rest of the night. Christopher, aware of her pain, never checked on her.

Summer mustered the strength to pull herself out of the tub the following morning. She needed to know if she had lost her baby. Christopher had already left the house, leaving her phone and car keys on the counter. So, she drove herself to the ER, where an ultrasound and examination confirmed her miscarriage.

Summer texted Ebony from the parking lot and waited in her SUV until Ebony's lunch break. When Ebony approached the car, she saw Summer's swollen face and puffy red eyes. Overwhelmed by the sight of Summer, Ebony walked away, trying to compose herself before facing her. She became emotional, knowing that it wasn't good news. Ebony opened the driver's door, and Summer leaned into her arms.

Summer cried out, "He killed my baby, Ebony. He killed my baby!" She repeated it over and over as Ebony held her and rocked her.

When Summer returned home, Christopher wasn't there. She walked into the bedroom and saw the trail of blood leading to the bathroom. Her bloody clothes were still on the bathroom floor. Instantly, she snapped. She began to pack clothes in a suitcase. She didn't know when Christopher would return, so she started snatching clothes from the drawers and hangers and putting them into her suitcase.

She threw clothes and shoes in her car. She pulled off her engagement ring and left it on the nightstand.

Summer called Ebony from the car and asked for a ride after she finished work. She gave Ebony directions to where she would be waiting. When Ebony picked her up, Summer transferred all her belongings to Ebony's car and left her keys and phone in the glove compartment of her SUV. She had Ebony drive her to her old apartment and surprised Mr. Ben with a visit. Mr. Ben was very upset when he saw all the bruises on her face; it was a tense moment as Summer had to talk him down from calling some of his old-school friends and showing up at Christopher's house.

She stayed the night at Mr. Ben's apartment and had him rent her a car in his name, traveling one way. She knew Christopher had no clue that she had saved Miss Dangerfield's home. She planned to return home with the intention of never returning.

The next day, Summer drove nonstop. She was so deep in sorrow that it was like an out-of-body experience. She was utterly exhausted and hadn't slept in three days. Finally, she made it home and called Mr. Jeffery to pick her up at the airport, where she returned the car rental. Mr. Jeffery was gravely concerned for her life. She looked like a battered, frail woman. He took her into his arms and walked her to the truck.

As they pulled into the driveway of her home, she could see Mimi's memorial tree waving in the wind as if she was welcoming her home. Mr. Jeffery had already arranged her bedroom furniture up in her old room from her apartment. However, she found herself drawn to Miss Dangerfield's room. She crawled into her bed, where she could still smell her sweet perfume on the blanket. Mr. Jeffery had washed the bedspread using a splash of Miss Dangerfield's perfume to keep her room smelling like her sweet presence. Summer remained in that spot for two days, sleeping. She refused to get out of bed and eat. Finally, Mr. Jeffery burst into the room using some of Miss Dangerfield's stern words and got her to eat a bowl of soup.

As she tried to sink back into the depths of her depressive thoughts, Summer could hear a tapping outside the window. The tapping became so annoying that she jumped up and snatched the curtains back to see what it was. To her surprise, it was a branch off Miss Dangerfield's memorial tree flapping in the wind and tapping on the window. Summer smiled and took that as a clear sign of Miss. Dangerfield telling her to get her tail out of that bed and pull herself together. So, Summer walked outside and looked up into the beautiful blue sky. Suddenly, a sweet-smelling breeze hit her face. It felt like a much-needed divine intervention. Summer laid under Mimi's tree, getting lost in the moment of peace, gazing at the beautiful sky attempting to find solace and comfort.

She was daydreaming of Miss Dangerfield holding and rocking her baby, saying, "Now, Summer, you have to get up and get on with your life. The baby and I are doing just fine."

In that instant, she felt relieved from the burden of guilt of not protecting her baby from Christopher, a guilt that had been weighing her down since the day she left. Before she knew it, she was being awakened by Mr. Jeffery.

"You have to get up off that ground, child. The bugs are going to eat you up. I really think you need to go see someone. This just not healthy, child."

Summer stood up, smiling at him, channeling Mimi. "Come on, Mr. Jeffery. I promise I'm fine. As long as I'm back home, I'm fine."

"I'll believe that when I stop seeing your bare bones through your skin."

Summer forced a smile and thanked him for caring for her. Later that evening, she called Mr. Ben and told him she'd wire him some money because she wanted him to purchase a burner phone and take it to Ebony. She really needed to find out if Christopher had accepted that it was over and had stopped looking for her.

## CHAPTER 21: REVISITING HER PAST

Mr. Jeffery told Summer they needed volunteers to read to the younger kids at the group home. He encouraged her to volunteer. Summer was hesitant about returning to the place that she felt caused her so much pain, but she would soon learn it brought her so much joy. There were so many kids to hug and show love to.

Summer started spending all her time volunteering wherever she could lend a hand. She found comfort in being around the kids. Besides, she had no idea if she'd ever be able to have another baby after the trauma she suffered from Christopher. Nevertheless, she wouldn't let her mind dwell on the bad moment. She kept herself busy, blocking out anything resembling the happiness she once felt.

Summer waited a week after talking to Mr. Ben before reaching out to Ebony. He had given her the phone number to the burner phone. Summer sent Ebony a text with two pink hearts from her new cell number. Ebony wasted no time calling the number back. Summer picked up and held the phone without saying hello. She needed to make sure it was Ebony calling.

"Summer," Ebony said, her voice carrying a hint of relief.

In a soft voice, she answered, "It's me, Ebony."

Letting her emotions overtake her, Ebony cried during the first five minutes of their call.

"I miss you so much, Summer. Please tell me you are okay."

"I'm better. I just have to take it one day at a time. I feel like he took so much from me."

Ebony urgently pleaded with her not to stay at Miss Dangerfield's home. She was terrified that Christopher would track her there.

"He's going crazy; he doesn't even look the same. He had someone falling me, Summer. Thomas had to fly out and talk directly to his father to save his company. Christopher is furious at me. He thinks I'm helping you hide and tried to sink Thomas's company. I discovered that he had eyes all over the hospital, and they were feeding him information.

"I love you, Summer. The thought of never seeing you again breaks my heart, but you need to keep moving. Mimi's house is not safe because it's in your name."

"I understand. Thanks for the information. I love you, bae," Summer said before ending the call.

"I love you, too, bae," Ebony said as she ended the call. Her love for Summer and knowing she was naive to Christopher's resources deepened her concerns.

Summer was convinced that she was safe. As far as Christopher knew, the house had gone into foreclosure. She even made sure to use two different moving companies when moving the furniture to Mimi's house. She left no stone unturned.

Summer was just getting into the groove of things. She'd picked some weight up and volunteered daily at the group home.

She finally felt some type of normalcy and had no plans to leave Mimi's house ever again.

*Dooms Day*

Summer was in the kitchen when she heard a knock on the door. It was dark outside, and the only visitors that stopped by were Mr. Jeffery's sons, and their visits were never unannounced. She peeped around the corner to look at Mr. Jeffery. He motioned for her to step back out of view.

"Who's there?" Mr. Jeffery asked.

"Hey, Mr. Jeffery. This is Christopher. I'm looking for Summer."

Her heart dropped, and she almost pissed her pants as she was paralyzed with fear; her body trembled uncontrollably.

"No, son, I haven't seen her," Mr. Jeffery yelled back through the door.

Summer tried to leave through the kitchen door, but her heart sank as she saw the glint of flashlights. There were men with flashlights patrolling the property. She knew it wasn't going to end well, and she wasn't going to allow anyone to hurt Mr. Jeffery. She was determined to protect him at all costs.

"Say, Mr. Jeffery... Why don't you just open up? I can see her car parked out in the driveway," Christopher said.

"Yes, that's correct. Summer had that car delivered sometime last year. Now you go ahead on, you hear."

Summer exhaled when she heard the screen door slam shut. Suddenly, she heard a loud crashing noise and glass shattering as Christopher kicked the door in. He walked into the house, charging for Mr. Jeffery.

"Look here, old man! Are you ready to lose your life?"

At that moment, Summer ran out of the kitchen.

"Please, no, don't hurt him."

"Summer, get back!" Mr. Jeffery yelled. "It'll be over my dead body that he will take you out of this house."

He attempted to struggle with Christopher as Summer stepped in the middle of them. She knew that one hit from Christopher could kill Mr. Jeffery.

Christopher had armed bodyguards with him as if he was coming to battle. He demanded that she come outside and speak with him. He grabbed her aggressively and forced her onto the porch. He demanded that she go pack her bags and discouraged Mr. Jeffery from calling the police. He said that he would burn Mimi's house down with Mr. Jeffery in it.

"Okay, Christopher, please. He has nothing to do with this. I promise he doesn't even know what's going on."

"Go now, Summer!" he yelled.

She quickly ran into the house, only grabbing her purse and stuffing a picture of her and Miss. Dangerfield inside it.

Then, she returned to the living room and told Mr. Jeffery, "I'm going back home with Christopher now. I'm fine. Please don't involve the police."

She feared for his life if he did.

"No," Mr. Jeffery said as she proceeded out the door.

He fell to his knees, begging and pleading with Christopher to leave Summer.

"Son, please just gone on about your business and let Ms. Summer be."

Christopher ignored his pleas as he walked out and told the armed men to make sure Mr. Jeffrey didn't try to call the police. Summer notice that the men were staying behind, so she violently fights and pulls away from Christopher.

She screamed, "Make them leave! No, don't hurt him! Make them leave."

He slammed her in the car and showed her a gun on his waist side. This made her calm down, but she continued begging him not to hurt Mr. Jeffery.

"Nobody's going to hurt that old fool," Christopher said as he slammed her door.

Summer, her face hidden in her hands, sobbed uncontrollably. She was engulfed by the fear of the unknown and accepted her fate. Christopher's eyes were ablaze with fury, and she knew she was as good as dead. As they drove away from the house, she watched it slowly vanish from her sight. She knew in her heart she'd never see her home again.

"You're a lying bitch!" he yelled. "You lied to me about everything. Did you really think I wouldn't find out that you have a deed in your damn name? Your bank statement came to the house, and you're still paying car insurance for a supposedly sold vehicle. You lie with a straight face, huh? Don't you? Because you're a liar!" he yelled.

Summer refused to respond as she sat in the passenger seat, wailing while he pulled her hair and pressed her face against the car's console. He noticed a road with a no-trespassing sign, so he reversed the car and drove down the dark road. Summer was very familiar with her surroundings and knew that the rocky pavement dirt road led to miles of green pastures with no help in sight. He abruptly parked the car and yelled for her to get out.

"Summer refused," thinking to herself if he was going to shoot her and leave her for dead, she wouldn't make it easy for him.

With the headlights beaming, revealing a dirt road and no homes in sight, Christopher knew he had her isolated.

When Summer refused to exit the car, he snatched two hands full of her hair and pulled her across the center console onto the ground. He then dragged her to the front of the car. She could feel her neck pop as he snatched her by her hair with such force. She was in pain from her rib cage hitting the rocky dirt pavement as he yanked her from the car to the ground. She could feel the cuts to her knees and thighs as he dragged her over the jagged texture of rocks. Summer screamed until she started to lose her voice.

"I told you, until death do us part. I will kill you before I let you go."

He put the gun to her mouth and screamed for her to open it as he stuck the barrel in her mouth.

"Do you want to die? I will kill both of us right here tonight."

Summer's body went limp as she accepted that this was how she would die. She stopped putting up a fight.

"Summer, why did you leave me?" Christopher screamed as he fell to his knees, holding the gun to his head. "How could you walk out on everything we built? You just walked away and left me like I meant nothing to you."

Summer let out a loud cry, "You killed my baby! How could you do that to our child? You just left me lying on the floor in my own blood, screaming while our baby was being torn from my womb."

This only infuriated Christopher more. It was like he was competing for her love with an unborn embryo. He yanked her up and threw her on top of the hot hood of the car.

"Who have you been fucking?" he screamed as he started to rip her clothes off while forcing himself inside of her.

She tried with all her might to fight him off. Summer felt as if she was being beaten and raped by a stranger. The Christopher she fell in love with disappeared. He had a look of rage in his eyes as if he were a junky who needed his fix, and Summer was the drug he craved so desperately for. After he had his way with her, he patted her on the head and told her that it felt like their very first time. Summer turned her head to the side and couldn't look at him. He helped her off the hood of the car.

"Baby let's just go home, please. I will make it better."

Just like that, he was calm and trying to comfort her as if he wasn't the cause of her pain. As he helped her back in the car, Summer could feel the grit in her eyes. Her body was stinging and burning from cuts and abrasions. She was trembling with fear as she attempted to cover her exposed body. Christopher had ripped her clothing into pieces as he sexually relieved himself in her.

He drove them to a secluded private airport where his father's private jet waited to fly them back to Illinois. Christopher pulled up next to the vehicle that had been parked in Miss Dangerfield's driveway when the two bodyguards stepped out. He warned her not to get out of the car as he got out to talk to the pilot. Summer watched from afar as he and the pilot seemed to be in a disagreement. Christopher was walking back to the car, yelling on the phone.

"Dad, it's just me, Summer, and a few security details."

He yanked the passenger door open and demanded her to give him her identification. Then, he and the pilot boarded the plane. After about ten minutes, he returned with a silk robe, towels, and bottles of water that he got from the plane. He demanded that she clean herself up and put the robe on. He then went to the trunk of the car and retrieved his traveling bag, removing a pair of men's pajama pants from the bag and threw them in her lap. She dressed and exited the car with his pajama pants pulled up under her breasts, wearing a robe, and walking barefooted.

Christopher had personally combed her hair by raking it into her face to hide as much of her face as possible. He blocked the pilot from greeting Summer. He knew she was too afraid to go against him because she didn't know if Mr. Jeffery and Miss Dangerfield's house was safe. She dropped her head and took her seat as instructed. The only thing she whispered to Christopher was if she could use his phone to call and check on Mr. Jeffery. He didn't even acknowledge her. He immediately fell asleep when the plane took off, as if he had not slept in days. Summer stared out into the night skies; all she could think of was Mr. Jeffery and his safety. She would never forgive herself if something happened to him.

At some point during the flight, she had fallen asleep and was awakened by the bump of the wheels hitting the runway. Christopher was also awakened from the hard landing. He jumped and grabbed her arm as if she were attempting to run away.

The pilot stepped out of the cockpit to greet them as they exited. Christopher pushed Summer behind him, demanding her to keep her head down. However, she purposely made eye contact with the pilot, praying that he'd somehow rescue her. He stood in shock as he looked her up and down. He noticed that she didn't have any shoes on. He also saw the bruising to her face and body.

When they stepped off the plane, Christopher realized that she was dragging behind, so he pulled her as he walked at full speed. When he noticed that she was limping and couldn't keep up, he swooped her in his arms and carried her to the car he had waiting.

They arrived at the home she had prayed she would never have to see again. All the feelings of sorrow that she had attempted to overcome the last few weeks flooded back in. Her mind replayed the screams of the physical and emotional pain that she endured on her last night there. It was too much for her to handle, and she broke down in tears, falling to the floor. Christopher picked her up and carried her to the bathroom. He allowed her to cry out without threatening her from her outburst of sorrow. After undressing her slowly, as if he were concerned about her bruised and injured body, he turned on the shower and helped her in.

Summer immediately jumped back as the water stung when it hit her open cuts. Without hesitation, Christopher jumped in, fully clothed, to assist with bathing her. He took the towel to clean her face and dabbed gently as she winced in pain with every touch. He gently washed her hair as he could feel every lump he had caused. Resting his forehead on hers, he broke down in tears. He was weeping and pleading for her forgiveness. With no reaction to his pity cry, Summer shed tears of hopelessness. After her shower, she sat on the bed with her head down as Christopher bent down in front of her, grabbing her by the waist.

"Baby, you literally ripped my heart out when you disappeared. Just allow me to show you how much I regret mistreating you," he said as he looked up at her, making eye contact and gently kissing her body.

"I want what you want, Summer. I want us to have a family. We will move to Bora Bora for a few months, work on us, and work on starting our family. I will change and do whatever it takes to make you happy. Please give me a chance, baby, please."

Not addressing his plea for forgiveness, Summer asked, "Can I call and check on Mr. Jeffery?"

Christopher walked downstairs and returned with her cell phone. Before she could dial Mr. Jeffery's number, she noticed several missed calls and texts from Ebony. The texts were urgent, almost frantic, and the missed calls were numerous. Summer wondered how Ebony knew she was back. She dialed Mr. Jeffrey's number to check on him. With fear in her heart with every unanswered ring, she almost leaped off the bed when he finally answered.

"Summer! he yelled. "Lord, baby girl, you have given me heart trouble. Are you okay, darling? Are you hurt?"

"I'm okay," she replied, eyeing Christopher.

"Just come home, Summer."

"I will. Are you hurt?"

He told her that the young men had actually helped him nail the door back up and that the phone she had left hadn't stopped ringing.

"It's that young lady Ebony. I'm sorry, but I told her what happened."

"It's okay. Just get some rest. I'm fine," Summer said in a weak, shaky voice, her hands trembling as she ended the call with Christopher snatching the phone away. Mr. Jeffery could hear in her voice that she was anything but fine.

Her voice, a fragile whisper, carried the weight of her fear and uncertainty, a stark contrast to her words of reassurance. She had been beaten and violated, her mind racing, not knowing what would end her life first—her injuries that clearly needed medical attention or at the hands of Christopher Diamond.

Summer could tell that Christopher hadn't been sleeping based on the bags under his eyes. As soon as his head hit the pillow, he was out with a grip on Summer, and she was forced to fall asleep in his arms. She woke up with a severe headache and dry mouth. So, she eased from under his clench and slid out of bed, and headed downstairs for Tylenol and water. She remembered that she had a bottle of Tylenol in her work bag in the office, so she went there and was shocked by the scene. Her entire life was spread out on the desk. Christopher had hired a private investigator, a discovery that filled her with fear and vulnerability. She found pictures of Ebony leaving home and work, all of her financial records, a copy of the title to her car, and the deed to her house.

There was never a reason for her to hide in the kitchen at her home. When Christopher knocked on the door, he already knew she was there. There were photos of her and Mr. Jefferey at Miss Dangerfield's home from a week prior to him showing up. He even had Stevin monitored. In an envelope off to the side were IDs and passports with their pictures but different names. It was clear that Christopher had other plans for them. She walked out of the office and through the family room. There, she found pictures of herself all over the floor and table. Boxes of tissues, a waste basket full of used tissue, and all her photos were by his favorite chair. The room looked as if he'd sat in one spot mourning over her photos.

Summer walked into the kitchen to get a glass of water. As she stood drinking the water, she heard Christopher scream out her name. He startled her, and she dropped the glass. It broke, and water splashed everywhere. Christopher heard the glass shatter and ran downstairs as Summer attempted to clean up the broken glass from the floor. She looked up and saw him running towards her with a gun in his hand.

"No!" she screamed as she backed into the corner, holding both hands in the air as if she could block a bullet. "I was just getting water!"

In a rage, he snatched her up and dragged her upstairs, demanding her back to bed. He sat up in the bed with a look of desperation as if he could lose everything in any second. He finally turned off all the lights and laid back down. Afraid to move, Summer stared out into the dark, feeling hopeless about life and a better outcome.

The following morning, Christopher was jolted awake by a phone call that left him in an uproar. The call made him so agitated that he was willing to leave Summer alone at the house. He started pacing back and forth around the bed.

"Summer, I swear before God, if you leave this house, I will destroy everybody you love and make you watch."

He pulled her by her arm and forced her to spread her fingers as he slid her engagement ring back on. Then, he squeezed her fingers together like a vice grip. Summer screamed out in pain, begging Christopher to stop. He let her go only to throw her back onto the bed and climb on top of her, threatening to kill her if she was not there when he came home. He walked around the house, removing all the phones, taking the power cords from the computer, and even taking all the car keys. Then, he rushed out of the house after packing up the office, unaware that Summer had already seen his previous activities and plans for them

# CHAPTER 22: A WAY OUT

Summer laid in bed sobbing; she couldn't continue life like this any longer. She had contemplated her escape throughout the night, knowing the only way out and to protect the ones she loved was death. She dragged her beaten, bruised body throughout the house, finding any bottle of medicine she could use to make a lethal cocktail. She grabbed all the pill bottles and a bottle of water and returned upstairs. She also grabbed her and Mimi's picture before going into the master bathroom and sitting on the floor. She felt like she needed to end her life in the same place she allowed Christopher to end the life of her child.

She took a towel and emptied all the pills into the towel. She stared at the photo as she rocked back and forth, crying and pleading for her forgiveness. Summer's only goal at the beginning of this journey was to make Miss Dangerfield proud, and she felt like an epic failure.

"Forgive me, momma," she cried out as she rocked back and forth, holding the picture close to her heart.

"Momma, my body and mind can't take anymore. I can't endure it anymore. Why Lord? What did I do so wrong my entire life to be dealt this hand? Mimi, I'm sorry. I don't know any other way. Please help me, mom. Please show me a better way. If it's a better way, Lord, please show me a way out."

Summer sat in complete silence, praying for forgiveness for taking her own life. Then, she sat up and took a handful of pills in the palm of her hand. She opened a bottle of water and threw her head back to consume them. Just then, the doorbell rang. Afraid that it could be Christopher, she hid all the pill bottles under the cabinet, placing the handful of pills back into the towel.

"Shit, this may be Ebony," she thought. Fearing her life could be in danger, she wanted to get her away from the house before Christopher returned. Without bothering to get dressed, she ran downstairs and quickly snatched the front door open. She immediately stepped back and took a big gasp of breath in surprise at who was standing in front of her. It was Mr. Diamond, Christopher's father.

"Oh no, it's worse than what my pilot described. I'm here to set you free, Summer. The only way to save my son is to make you disappear."

Summer looked frightened; her eyes widened in fear, her mind racing, thinking, "Now his father is about to take me out. Is this the other way out?"

Mr. Diamond could see that she was confused and frightened.

He asked, "Do you want a way out? Do you seek a way to escape my son?"

She was scared, thinking this was a test from Christopher, so she didn't reply.

"We don't have much time, Summer. I've made plans that will keep Christopher busy only for a short while. I've become aware of all his extra activities he's been involved in, using all my resources. This is not the first time I've had to step in and bail my son out, but nothing to this extent. I don't know what hold you have on him, but if he's willing to go to these depths to keep a hold on you, something is not right mentally.

"My son needs help. Christopher was involuntarily committed when he was younger due to anger and violent outbursts. He never forgave me for having him committed. Once he turned twenty-one, Christopher moved as far as he could to get away from the family. He wants nothing to do with me but chooses to benefit from my power. All I need to know is do you want a way out? The situation is urgent, and we need to act quickly."

He handed her a large envelope and a duffel bag.

"In this envelope is your new life - a new identity, passport, and enough money to start a brand-new life without any worries. I have made it so that my son will never be able to trace you under your new identity. Just know if you take this opportunity, you must walk away from everything and everyone you love. As of today, Summer Taylor is dead," he said.

Summer was still confused and hesitant, so he took her by the hand.

"Come, let's sit. I know you love my son, but his obsession with you is unhealthy. Yes, his heart will be broken, but I'd rather see him heartbroken instead of in jail or dead. If you're denying this opportunity because you're holding on to any possibility of genuine love from my son, let me make this decision easier for you."

He placed a second envelope on the sofa next to her.

"Summer, did you ever wonder why Christopher was so adamant about keeping you away from me? I have been trying to talk to you for over three years now. I was giving my son a chance to do the right thing and make it right. Instead, he has dodged the conversation, lied, and manipulated all of us. Did he ever tell you that he had you investigated before ever taking you out on a date?"

"No, Summer said as her eyes widened."

"Well, he did by using my office to have one of my best PIs to research you. He learned more about you than you have ever known about yourself. When my son came to California for his birthday event, he sat me down and told me that he had found true love, and his intentions were to make you his wife. He spoke highly of you, but when I asked about your family, he fed me the same story you told. You see, the problem with that is he had no idea that I knew what he knew because everything he does ends up on my desk. So, your report ended up on my desk. I chose not to meet you the night of the party because I refused to look you in your eyes and lie to you. I was giving him time to inform you of what he knew. He called and told me that you had no interest in learning anything about your past and birth parents.

"When I summoned you guys back to California, he caused such a scene in the restaurant, and you and I never had the time to talk. My son sabotaged any communication with you. He even threatened to take his own life. His mom and my oldest son made a surprise trip to check on him because he sent everyone messages the day before, threatening to harm himself and you if we didn't back off. My son has kept information from you that would change your life. He's always known who your birth parents are."

Summer's heart sank; she couldn't believe what she was hearing. Mr. Diamond told her that Christopher had learned through his investigation who her parents were and that her mother was alive and living in Atlanta, Georgia. Her mother had not given her up willingly. She had gotten pregnant at thirteen and ran away from home with her seventeen-year-old boyfriend. They were homeless, living from house to house, and her father tried to sell drugs to earn money and was robbed and killed. It happened one night when her parents, along with their three-year-old daughter, were hanging out in an abandoned drug house. Her then sixteen-year-old mother decided to leave her with her father and went to the corner store, where she was when he was killed.

When she returned from the store, her mom found her boyfriend in the alley beside the house dead, with their daughter crying next to him while sitting in his blood. The emotional stress was too much, and her mom had a breakdown and ended up in the hospital. When she woke up, she learned that she had been listed as a runaway for three years, and her parents were at the hospital acting as her guardian. Her parents had given Summer up for adoption without ever meeting her and asked that all records be sealed. Summer's mother lost her and her father all in one night. She fell through the system, never being adopted, and became a ward of the state. Summer Taylor was the name she was given at birth by her parents.

Mr. Diamond touched her leg as she wept in disbelief. "If you're taking this opportunity, we must leave now."

Summer hurried upstairs and quickly changed into a pair of joggers and a T-shirt. She grabbed some items she had left at the home and placed them in a small duffle bag. Then, she snatched up her and Mimi's photo from the bathroom floor and placed her engagement ring on the nightstand. Summer hurried out the door with Christopher's father. Without time to think, she boarded Mr. Diamond's private plane with him and flew out to Missouri. He gave her detailed instructions, and Summer would choose her own destination at the next airport. She was given a burner phone to call her close friends to say goodbye and that she'd be leaving on her own accord without Christopher's knowledge, and this would be goodbye forever. She would have to destroy the burner phone and discard it at the airport.

He also gave her the envelope containing pictures and information about her parents and the option of opening it. If she chose to open the envelope, she would not be able to communicate with her mom. Christopher had her mom's information, so contacting her wouldn't be safe for Summer or her mother. Summer departed Mr. Diamond's plane and walked into the airport without a clue about her next move.

She was just handed an opportunity and learned at the same time that he kept the most important secret of her life from her, and she had to completely walk away from the truth she had yearned for so long. She called Mr. Jeffery and told him that she had to disappear forever and could never have any contact with him again. She also told him to look in the suitcase she had left. He found $160,000 in it. Summer had emptied her bank account on her first attempt to run. He was instructed to board the house for a couple of months and take a vacation until it was safe to return. She made him promise to keep Miss Dangerfield's home in his family and to make sure everyone knew that her tree was never to be cut down.

She couldn't bring herself to call Ebony, as she was heartbroken. Ebony had truly brought real joy and friendship into her life. Instead, she simply texted her two red hearts along with "I love you, Bae. I'm safe. Goodbye forever." After texting Ebony, she broke the phone in half, destroying it. Then, she sat in the airport, heartbroken and still contemplating whether she wanted to live life alone and broken.

As if it were a  clear sign from her beloved Mimi, an elderly lady took a seat beside her, and the familiar sweet scent of Mimi's perfume filled her nose. Glancing at her plane ticket and observing the elderly lady's destination, Summer made the decision to book the same flight.

As the plane started to pull away from the loading dock, flashes of her first time on the plane with Christopher flooded her mind. Her heart ached with the realization that her entire world, as she knew it, was over. She was still in love with the man she once knew as her knight in shining armor. She looked out the window at the serene, fluffy white clouds and the powder blue sky. Summer remembered the first time she beheld that view with Christopher by her side, as he kissed her cheek, telling her to open her eyes and look at that amazing view. As she stared out the window looking at the clouds, her eyes welled with tears that distorted her perfect view. Summer knew she was losing a lot, but at the same time, she was gaining everything!